MARVEL

# SPIDER-HAM

## A PIG IN TIME

AN ORIGINAL GRAPHIC NOVEL

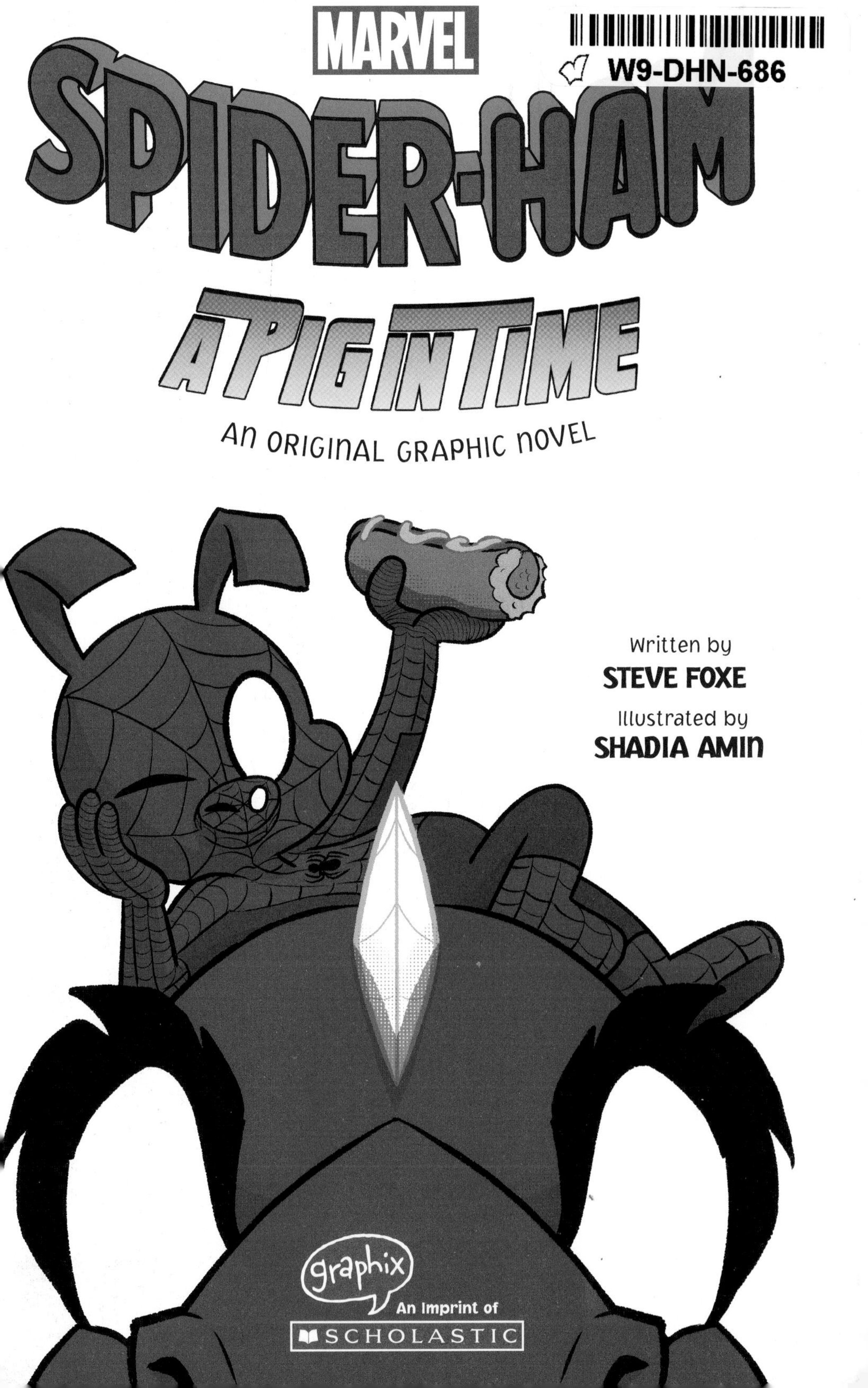

Written by
**STEVE FOXE**
Illustrated by
**SHADIA AMIN**

graphix
An Imprint of
SCHOLASTIC

ISBN 978-1-338-88943-7

10 9 8 7 6 5 4 3 2 1          23 24 25 26 27

Printed in the U.S.A.                    40

First edition, September 2023

Artwork by Shadia Amin
Edited by Conor Lloyd
Lettering by Rae Crawford
Book design by Ashley Vargas

Lauren Bisom, Senior Editor, Juvenile Publishing
Caitlin O'Connell, Associate Editor
Sven Larsen, VP Licensed Publishing
C.B. Cebulski, Editor in Chief

# CHAPTER ONE:
# OINK TO THE FUTURE!

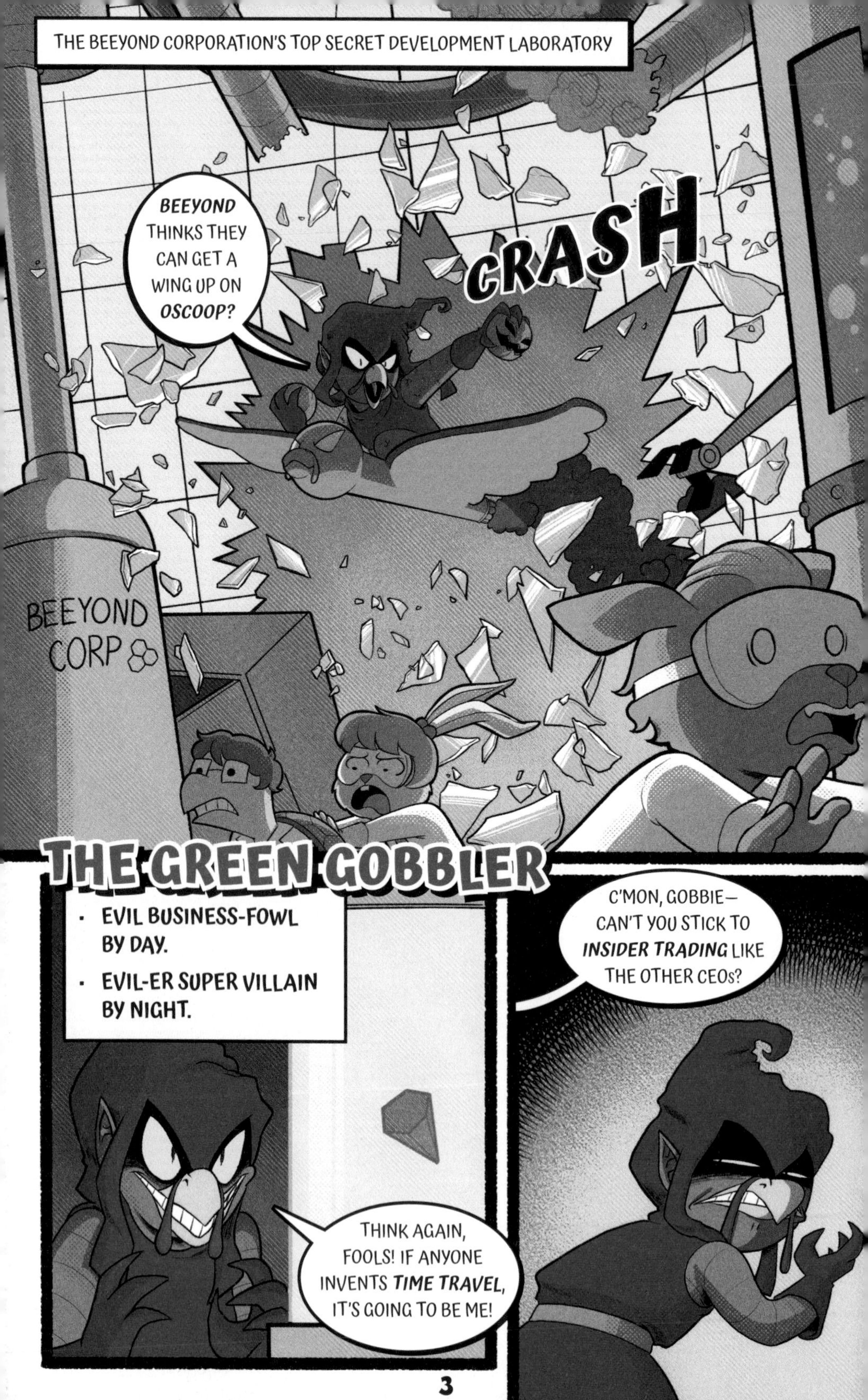
THE BEEYOND CORPORATION'S TOP SECRET DEVELOPMENT LABORATORY
BEEYOND THINKS THEY CAN GET A WING UP ON OSCOOP?
CRASH
BEEYOND CORP
THE GREEN GOBBLER
· EVIL BUSINESS-FOWL BY DAY.
· EVIL-ER SUPER VILLAIN BY NIGHT.
C'MON, GOBBIE— CAN'T YOU STICK TO INSIDER TRADING LIKE THE OTHER CEOs?
THINK AGAIN, FOOLS! IF ANYONE INVENTS TIME TRAVEL, IT'S GOING TO BE ME!

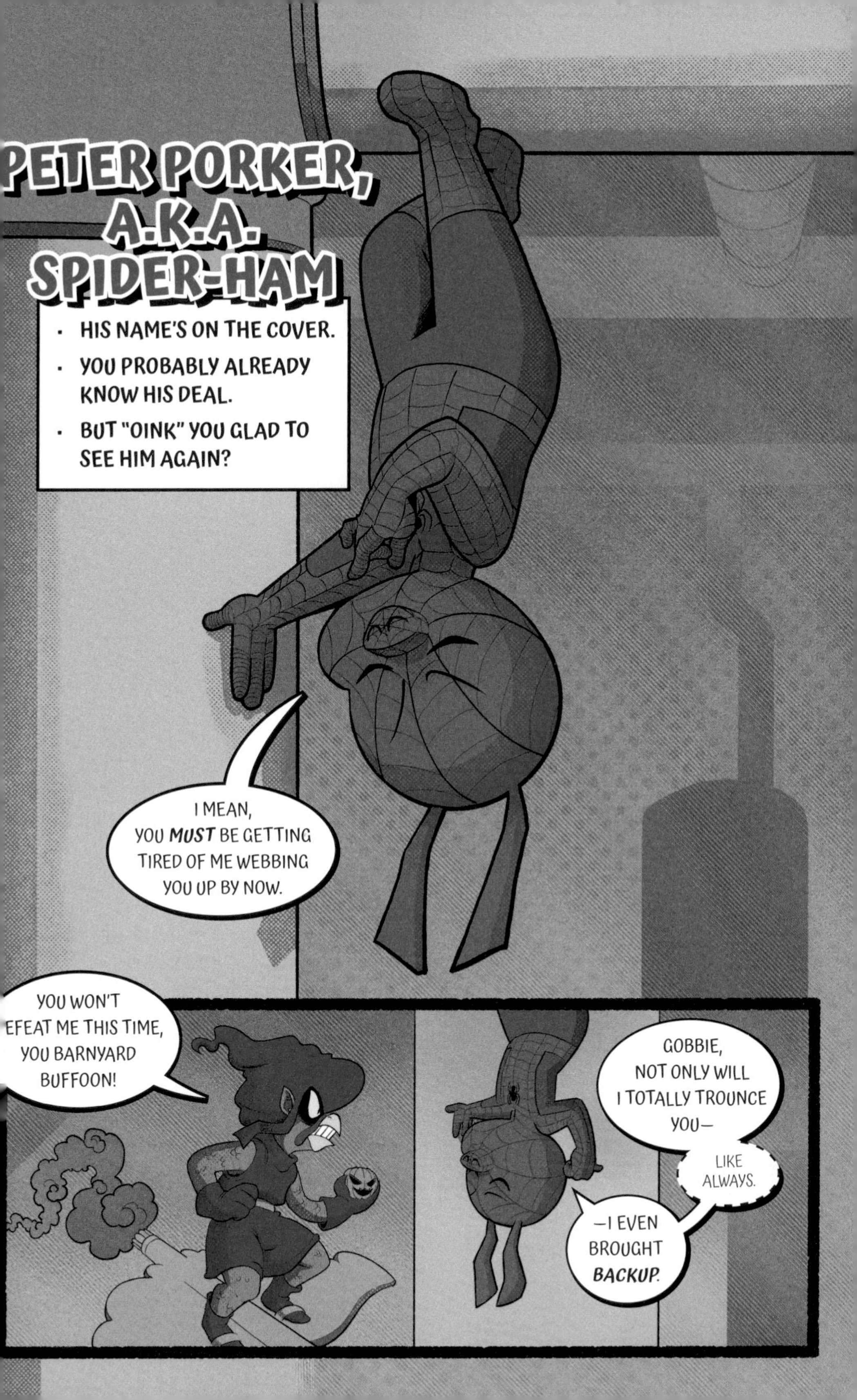

PETER PORKER, A.K.A. SPIDER-HAM
• HIS NAME'S ON THE COVER.
• YOU PROBABLY ALREADY KNOW HIS DEAL.
• BUT "OINK" YOU GLAD TO SEE HIM AGAIN?
I MEAN, YOU MUST BE GETTING TIRED OF ME WEBBING YOU UP BY NOW.
YOU WON'T EFEAT ME THIS TIME, YOU BARNYARD BUFFOON!
GOBBIE, NOT ONLY WILL I TOTALLY TROUNCE YOU—
LIKE ALWAYS.
—I EVEN BROUGHT BACKUP.

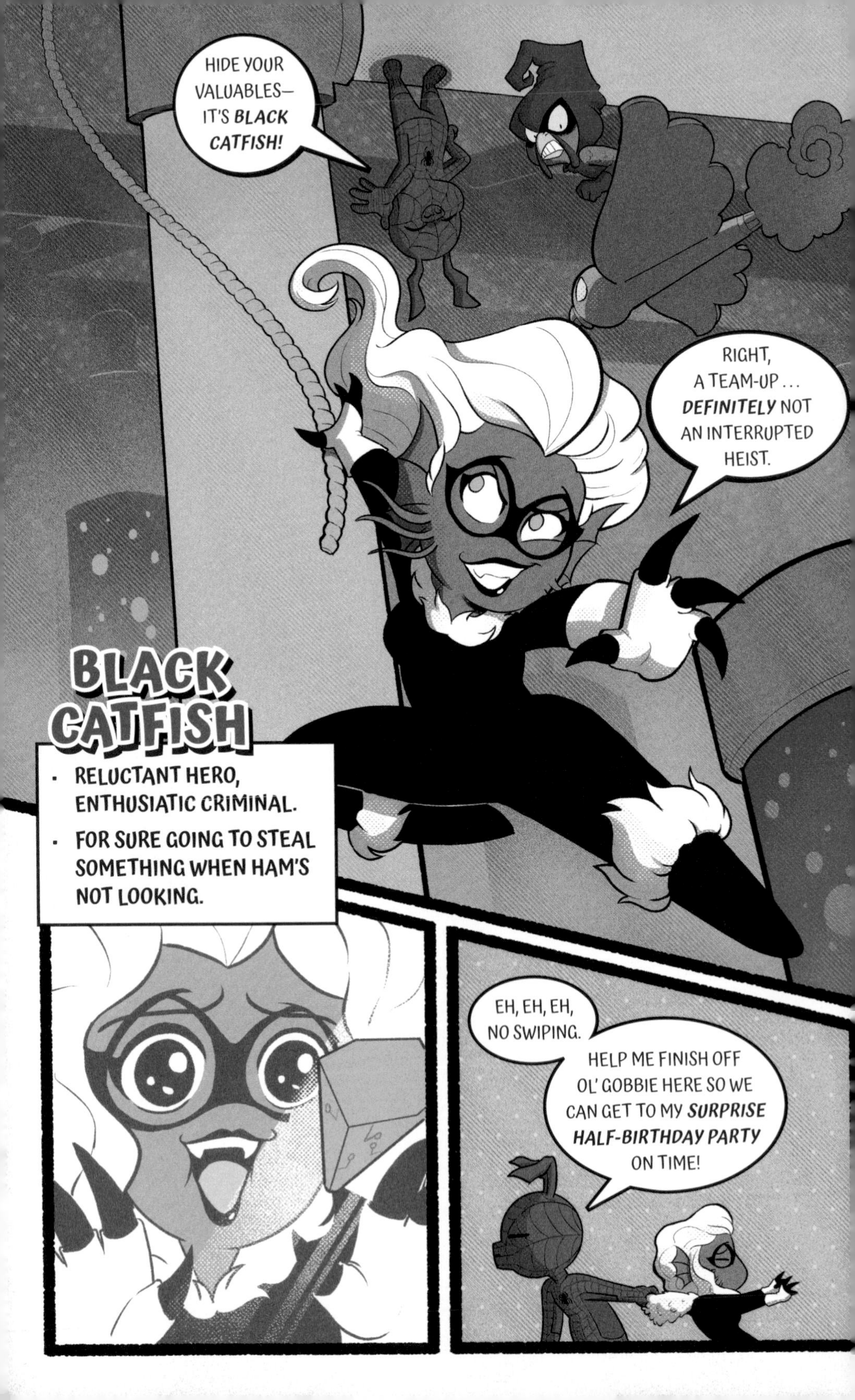
HIDE YOUR VALUABLES— IT'S BLACK CATFISH!
RIGHT, A TEAM-UP . . . DEFINITELY NOT AN INTERRUPTED HEIST.
BLACK CATFISH
• RELUCTANT HERO, ENTHUSIATIC CRIMINAL.
• FOR SURE GOING TO STEAL SOMETHING WHEN HAM'S NOT LOOKING.
EH, EH, EH, NO SWIPING.
HELP ME FINISH OFF OL' GOBBIE HERE SO WE CAN GET TO MY SURPRISE HALF-BIRTHDAY PARTY ON TIME!

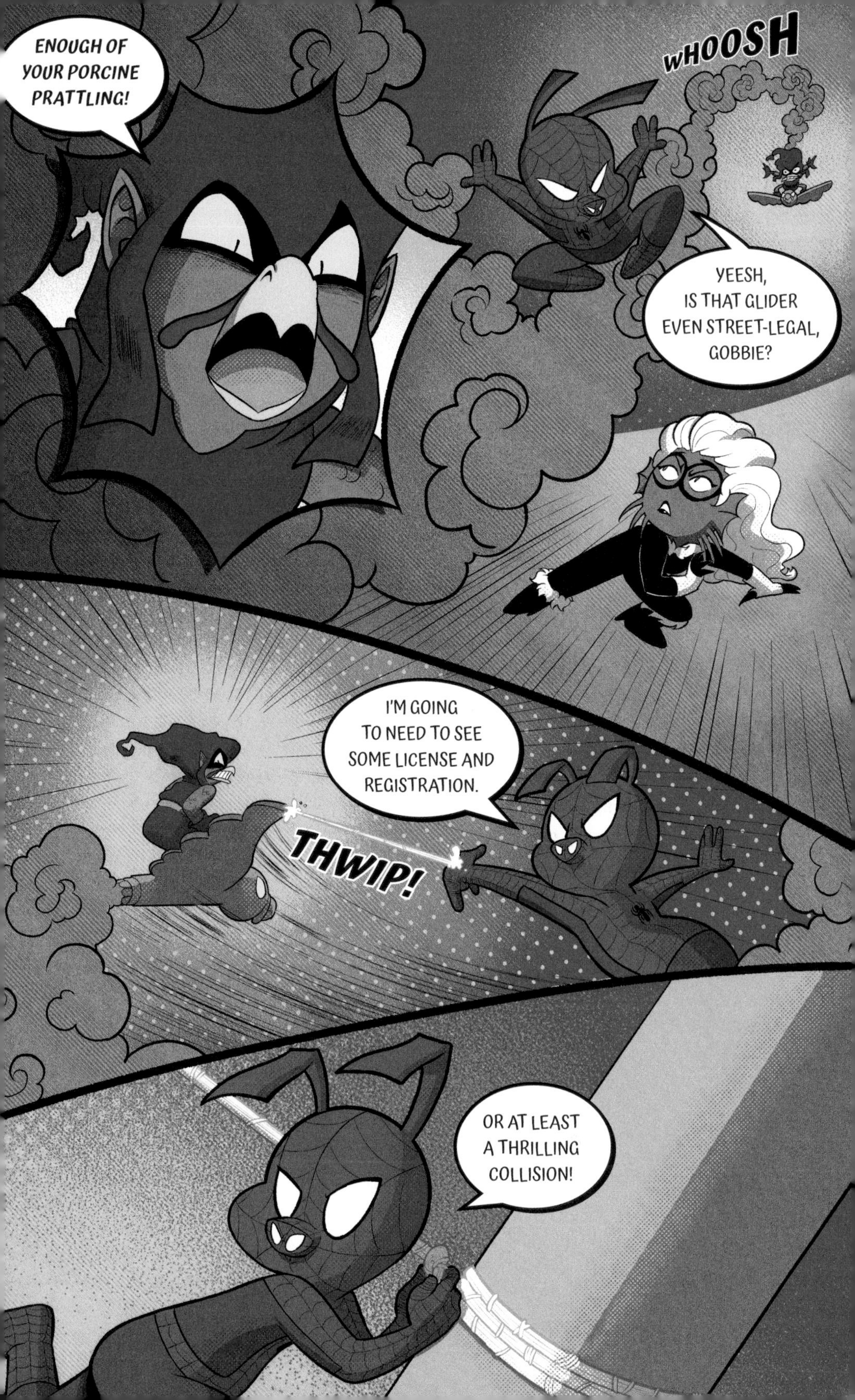
ENOUGH OF YOUR PORCINE PRATTLING!
WHOOSH
YEESH, IS THAT GLIDER EVEN STREET-LEGAL, GOBBIE?
I'M GOING TO NEED TO SEE SOME LICENSE AND REGISTRATION.
THWIP!
OR AT LEAST A THRILLING COLLISION!

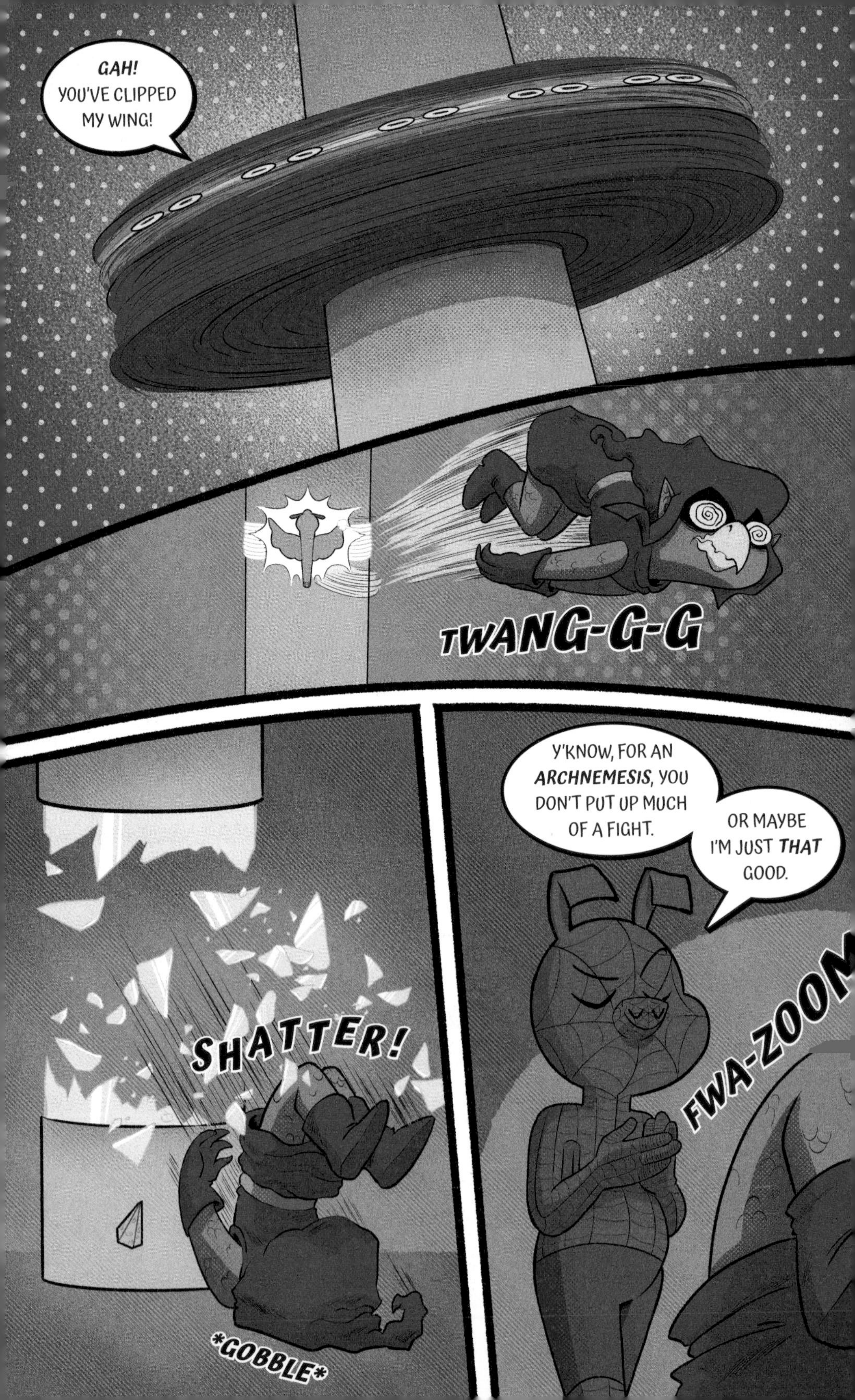
GAH! YOU'VE CLIPPED MY WING!
TWANG-G-G
SHATTER!
*GOBBLE*
Y'KNOW, FOR AN ARCHNEMESIS, YOU DON'T PUT UP MUCH OF A FIGHT.
OR MAYBE I'M JUST THAT GOOD.
FWA-ZOOM

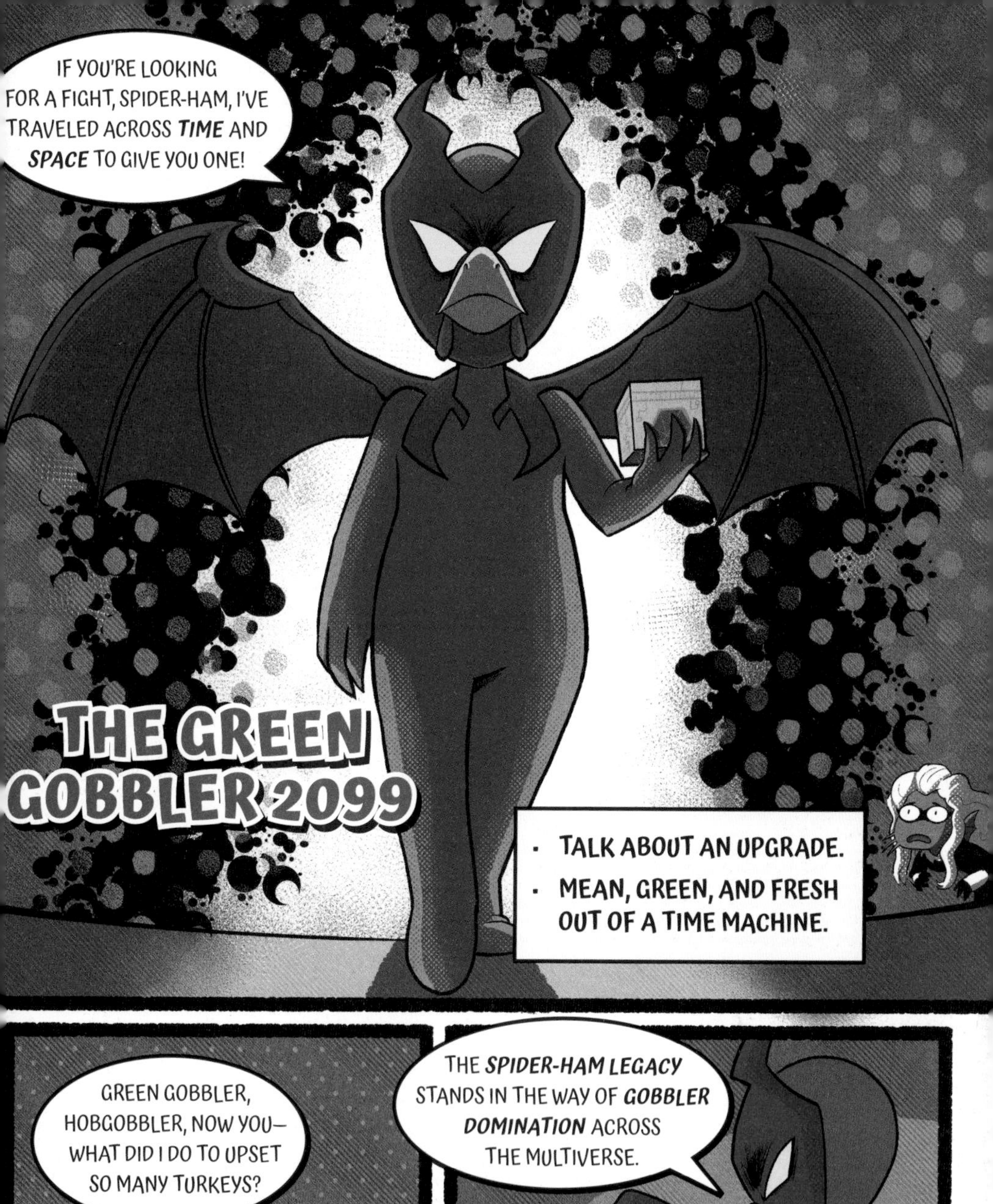
IF YOU'RE LOOKING FOR A FIGHT, SPIDER-HAM, I'VE TRAVELED ACROSS *TIME* AND *SPACE* TO GIVE YOU ONE!
THE GREEN GOBBLER 2099
• TALK ABOUT AN UPGRADE.
• MEAN, GREEN, AND FRESH OUT OF A TIME MACHINE.

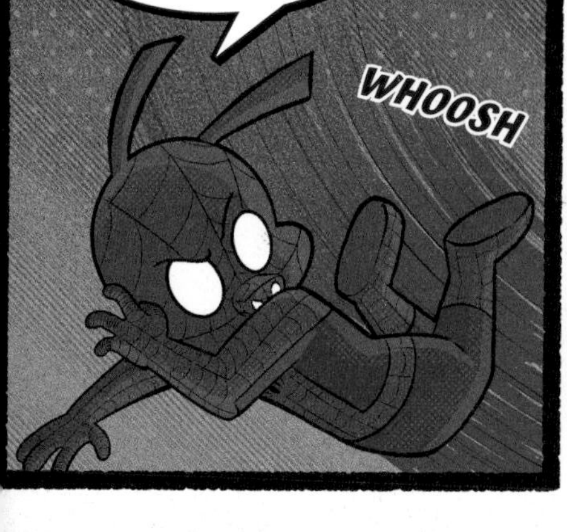
GREEN GOBBLER, HOBGOBBLER, NOW YOU— WHAT DID I DO TO UPSET SO MANY TURKEYS?
WHOOSH

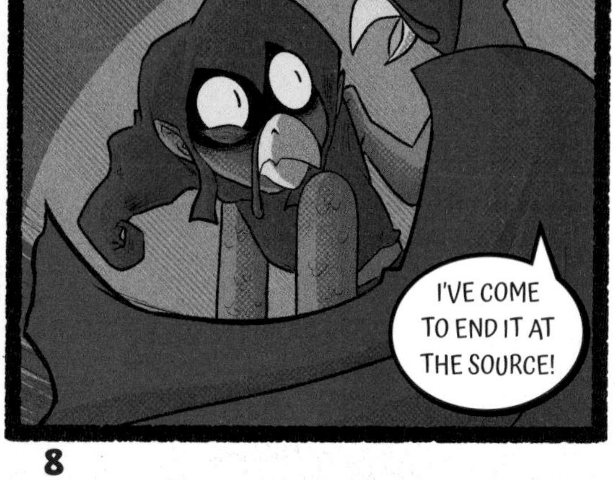
THE *SPIDER-HAM LEGACY* STANDS IN THE WAY OF *GOBBLER DOMINATION* ACROSS THE MULTIVERSE.
I'VE COME TO END IT AT THE SOURCE!

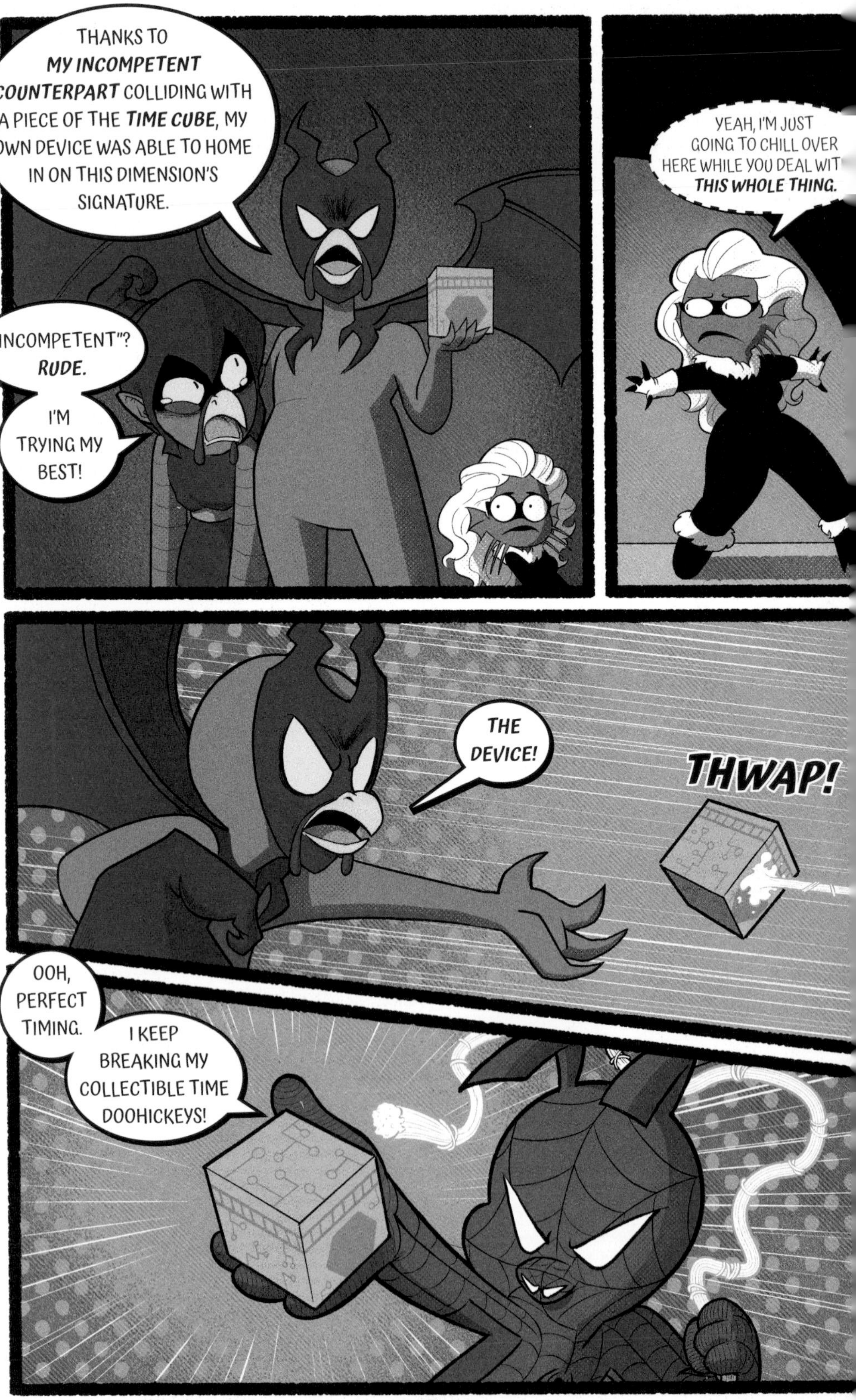
THANKS TO MY INCOMPETENT COUNTERPART COLLIDING WITH A PIECE OF THE TIME CUBE, MY OWN DEVICE WAS ABLE TO HOME IN ON THIS DIMENSION'S SIGNATURE.
"INCOMPETENT"? RUDE.
I'M TRYING MY BEST!
YEAH, I'M JUST GOING TO CHILL OVER HERE WHILE YOU DEAL WIT THIS WHOLE THING.
THE DEVICE!
THWAP!
OOH, PERFECT TIMING.
I KEEP BREAKING MY COLLECTIBLE TIME DOOHICKEYS!

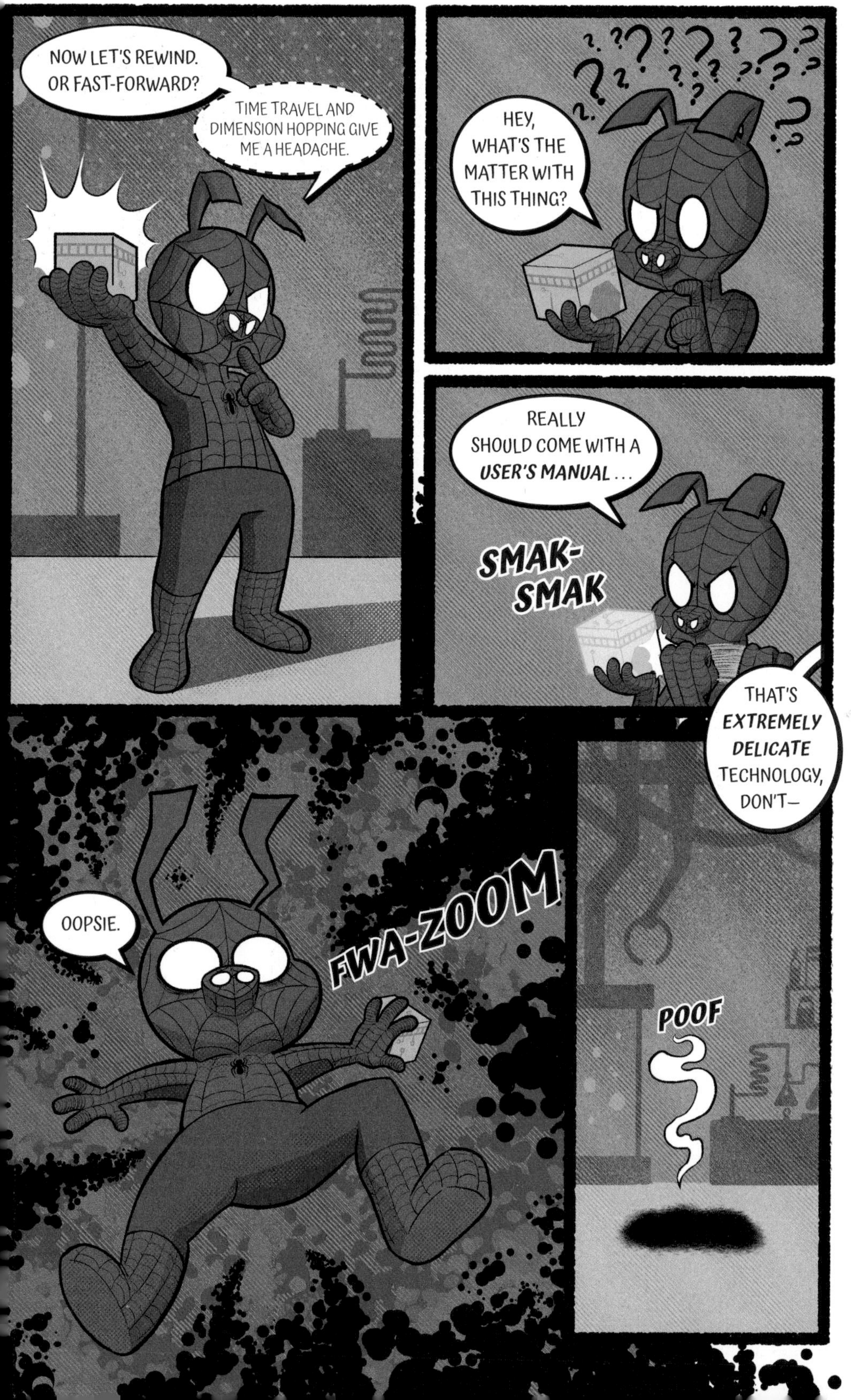
NOW LET'S REWIND. OR FAST-FORWARD?
TIME TRAVEL AND DIMENSION HOPPING GIVE ME A HEADACHE.
HEY, WHAT'S THE MATTER WITH THIS THING?
REALLY SHOULD COME WITH A USER'S MANUAL . . .
SMAK-SMAK
THAT'S EXTREMELY DELICATE TECHNOLOGY, DON'T—
OOPSIE.
FWA-ZOOM
POOF

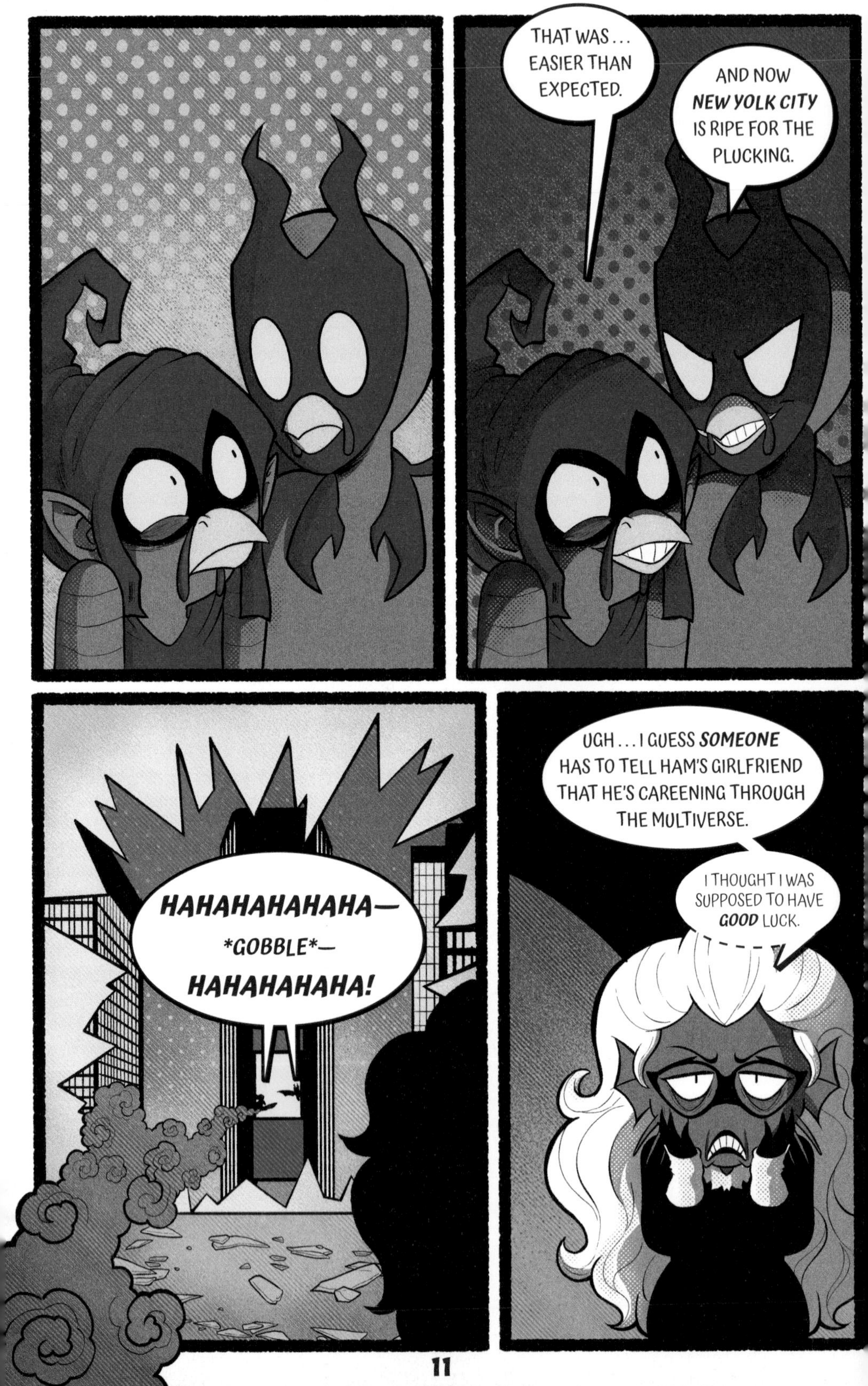
THAT WAS . . . EASIER THAN EXPECTED.
AND NOW ***NEW YOLK CITY*** IS RIPE FOR THE PLUCKING.
HAHAHAHAHAHA— *GOBBLE*— HAHAHAHAHA!
UGH . . . I GUESS ***SOMEONE*** HAS TO TELL HAM'S GIRLFRIEND THAT HE'S CAREENING THROUGH THE MULTIVERSE.
I THOUGHT I WAS SUPPOSED TO HAVE ***GOOD*** LUCK.

# CHAPTER TWO:

# A STITCH IN TIME SAVES SWINE!

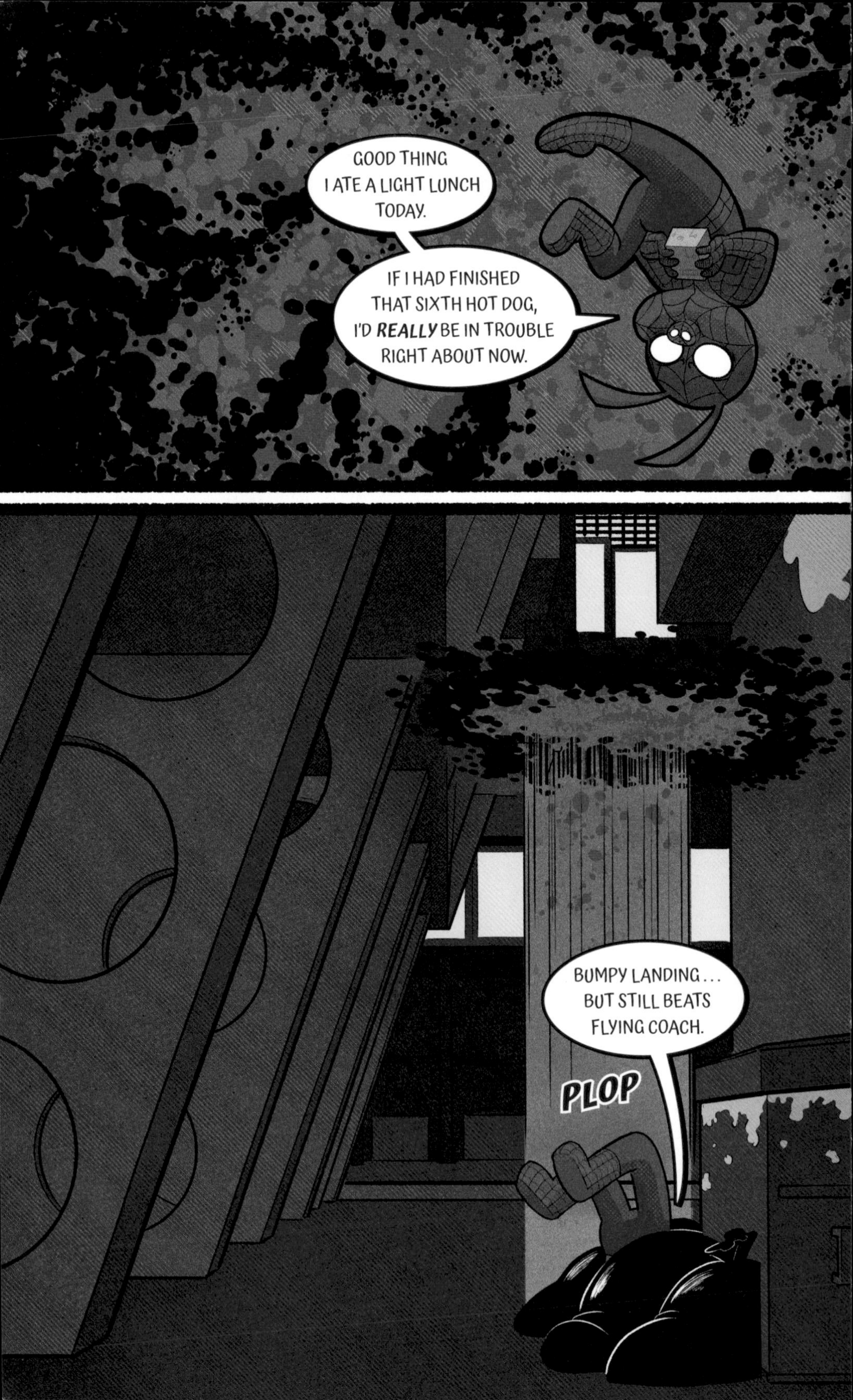
GOOD THING I ATE A LIGHT LUNCH TODAY.
IF I HAD FINISHED THAT SIXTH HOT DOG, I'D **REALLY** BE IN TROUBLE RIGHT ABOUT NOW.
BUMPY LANDING . . . BUT STILL BEATS FLYING COACH.
PLOP

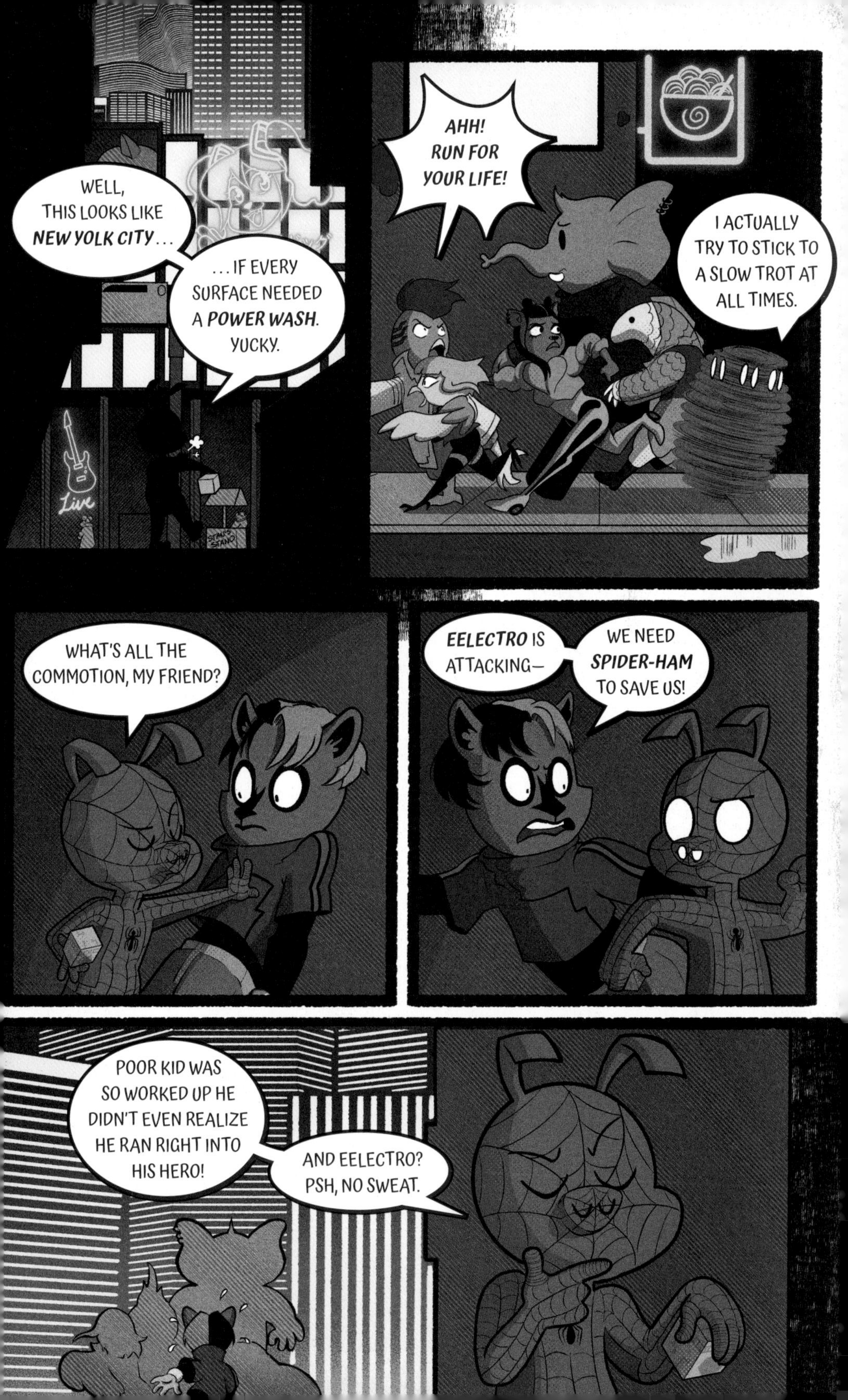
WELL, THIS LOOKS LIKE NEW YOLK CITY . . .
. . . IF EVERY SURFACE NEEDED A POWER WASH. YUCKY.
AHH! RUN FOR YOUR LIFE!
I ACTUALLY TRY TO STICK TO A SLOW TROT AT ALL TIMES.
WHAT'S ALL THE COMMOTION, MY FRIEND?
EELECTRO IS ATTACKING—
WE NEED SPIDER-HAM TO SAVE US!
POOR KID WAS SO WORKED UP HE DIDN'T EVEN REALIZE HE RAN RIGHT INTO HIS HERO!
AND EELECTRO? PSH, NO SWEAT.

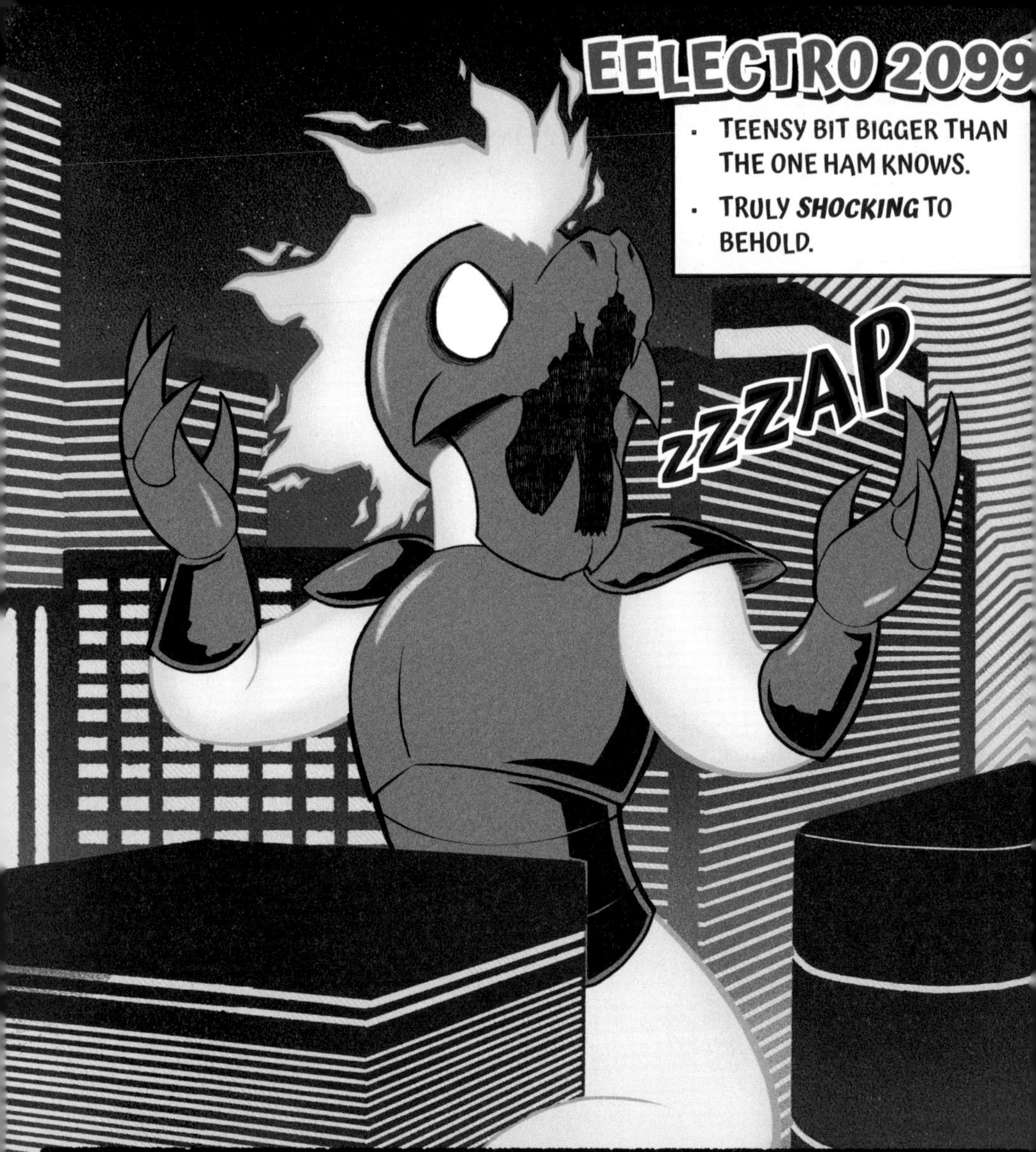
EELECTRO 2099
TEENSY BIT BIGGER THAN THE ONE HAM KNOWS.
TRULY SHOCKING TO BEHOLD.
ZZZZAP

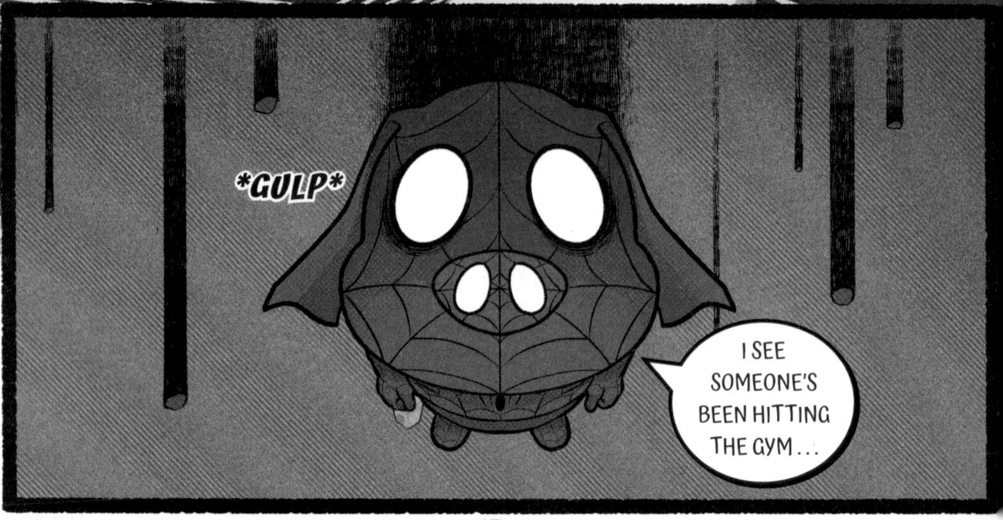
*GULP*
I SEE SOMEONE'S BEEN HITTING THE GYM . . .

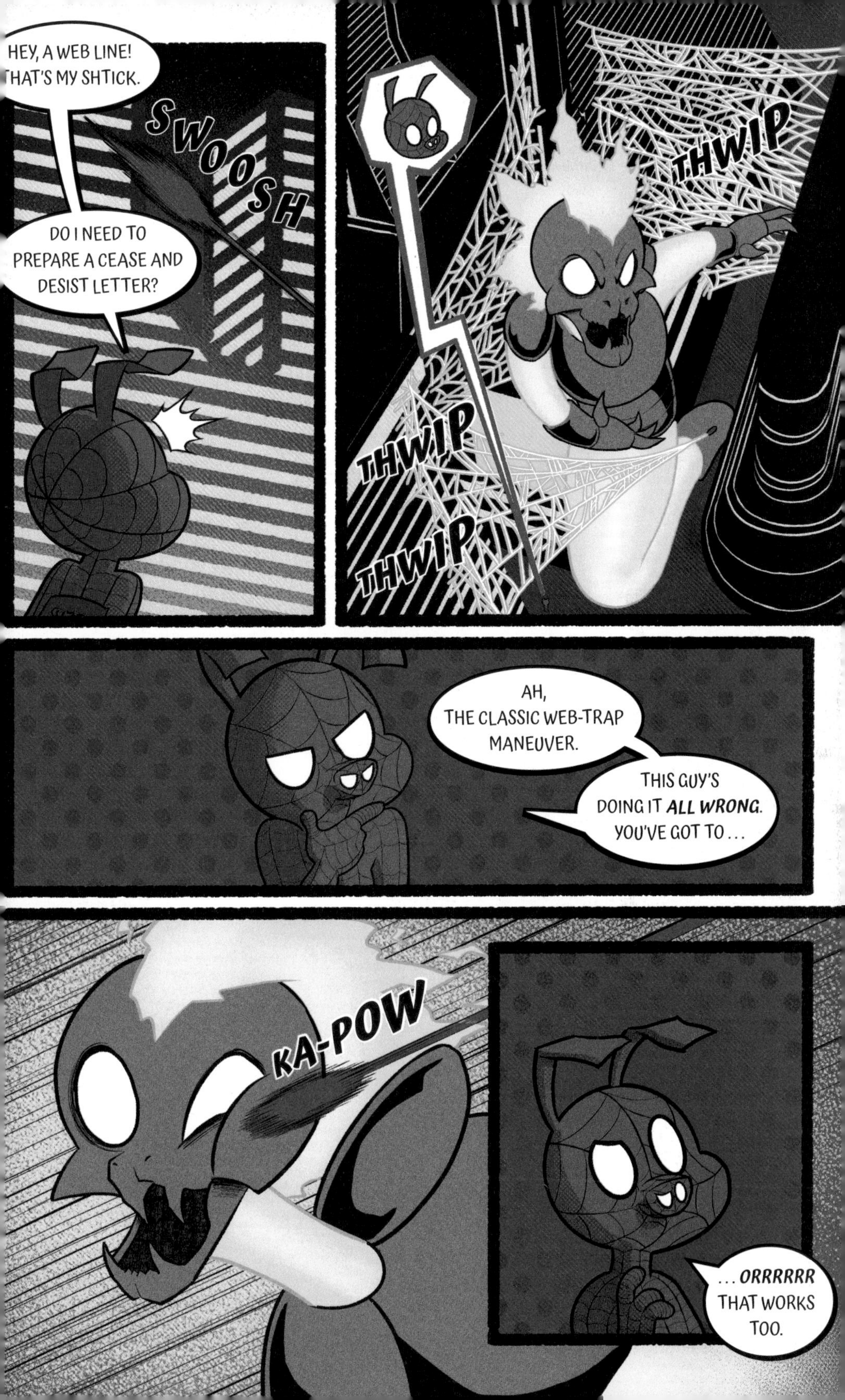
HEY, A WEB LINE! THAT'S MY SHTICK.
SWOOSH
DO I NEED TO PREPARE A CEASE AND DESIST LETTER?
THWIP
THWIP
THWIP
AH, THE CLASSIC WEB-TRAP MANEUVER.
THIS GUY'S DOING IT **ALL WRONG**. YOU'VE GOT TO . . .
KA-POW
. . . ***ORRRRRR*** THAT WORKS TOO.

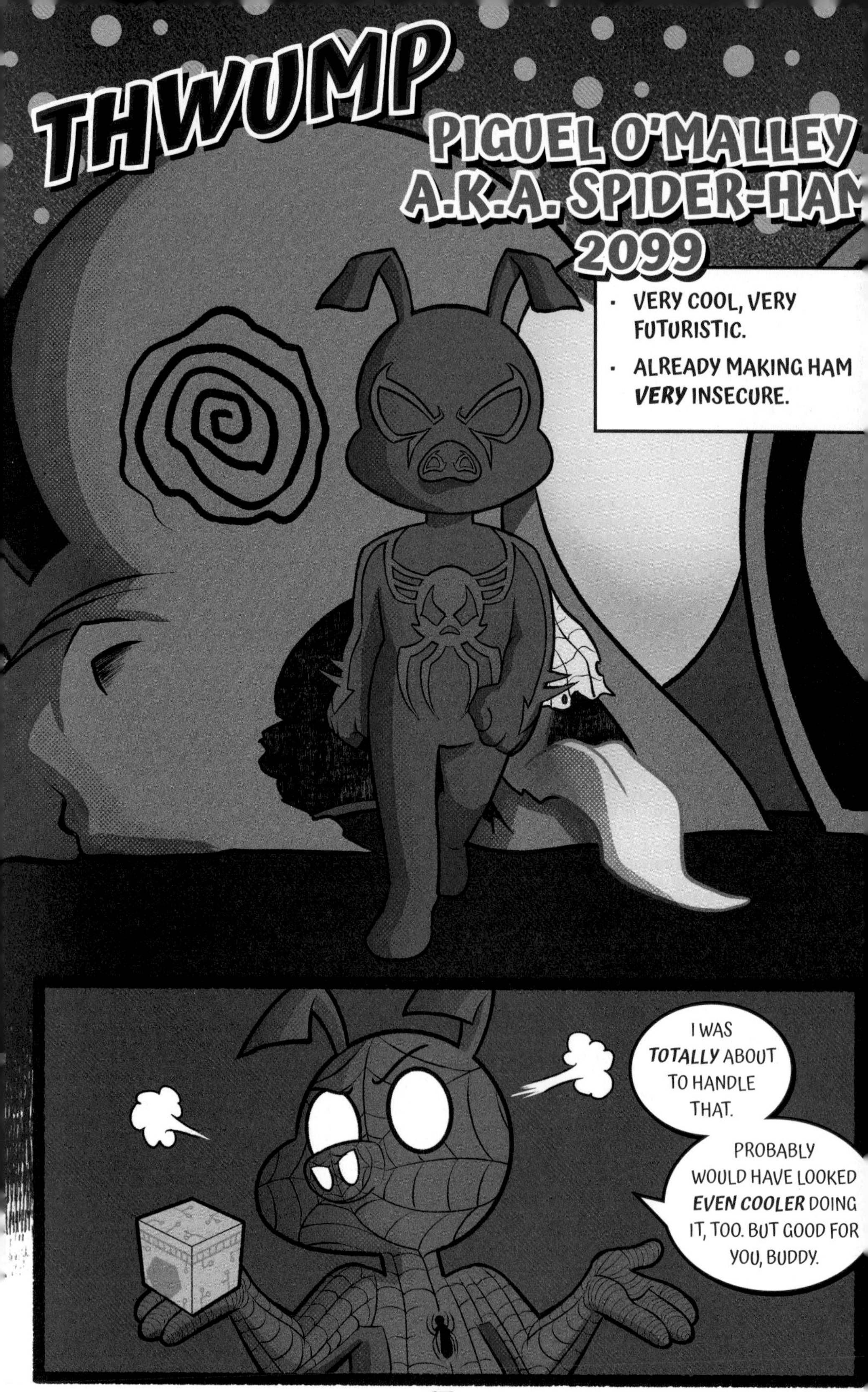
THWUMP
PIGUEL O'MALLEY
A.K.A. SPIDER-HAM
2099
• VERY COOL, VERY FUTURISTIC.
• ALREADY MAKING HAM ***VERY*** INSECURE.
I WAS ***TOTALLY*** ABOUT TO HANDLE THAT.
PROBABLY WOULD HAVE LOOKED ***EVEN COOLER*** DOING IT, TOO. BUT GOOD FOR YOU, BUDDY.

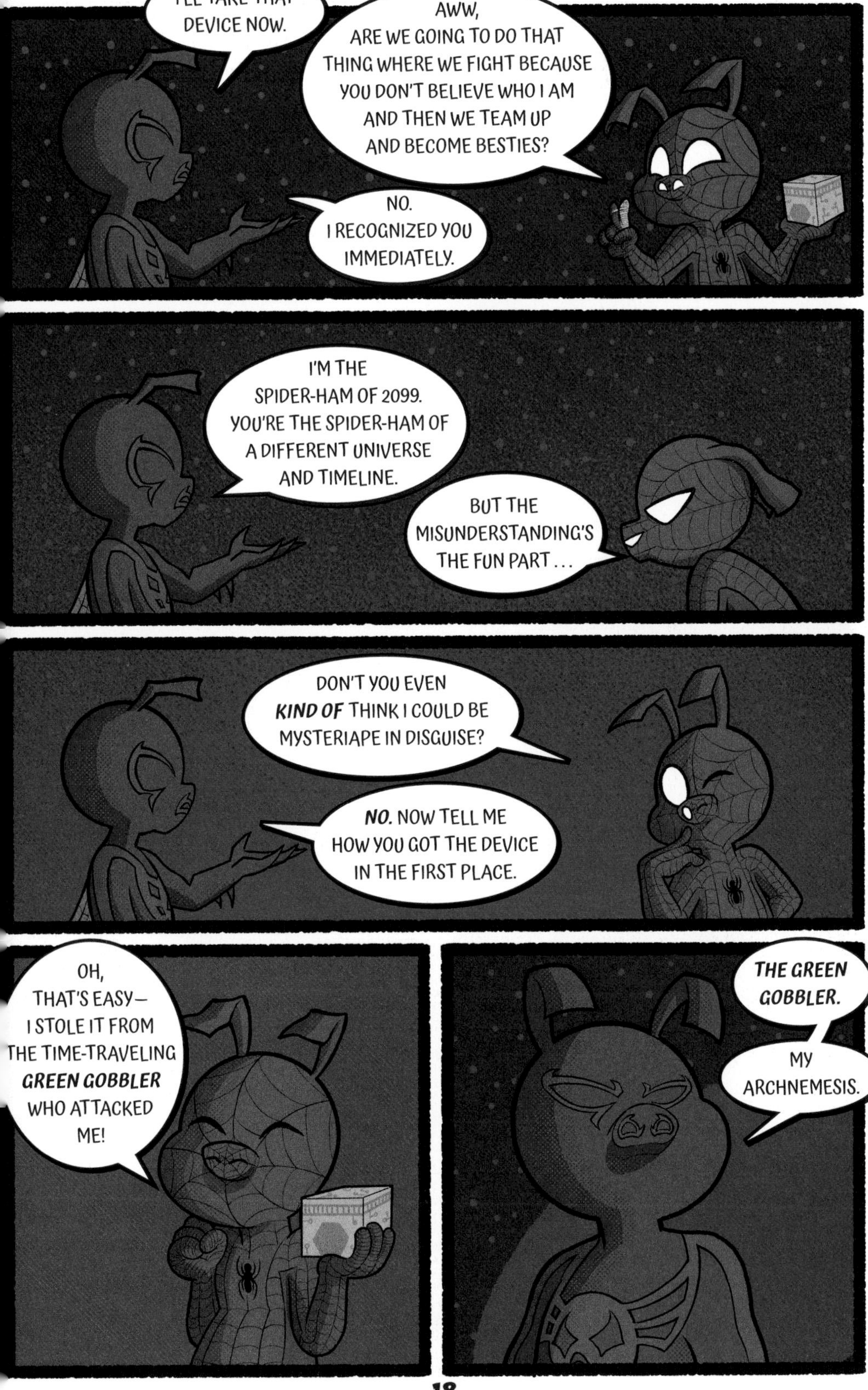
I'LL TAKE THAT DEVICE NOW.
AWW, ARE WE GOING TO DO THAT THING WHERE WE FIGHT BECAUSE YOU DON'T BELIEVE WHO I AM AND THEN WE TEAM UP AND BECOME BESTIES?
NO. I RECOGNIZED YOU IMMEDIATELY.
I'M THE SPIDER-HAM OF 2099. YOU'RE THE SPIDER-HAM OF A DIFFERENT UNIVERSE AND TIMELINE.
BUT THE MISUNDERSTANDING'S THE FUN PART . . .
DON'T YOU EVEN ***KIND OF*** THINK I COULD BE MYSTERIAPE IN DISGUISE?
***NO.*** NOW TELL ME HOW YOU GOT THE DEVICE IN THE FIRST PLACE.
OH, THAT'S EASY— I STOLE IT FROM THE TIME-TRAVELING ***GREEN GOBBLER*** WHO ATTACKED ME!
***THE GREEN GOBBLER.***
MY ARCHNEMESIS.

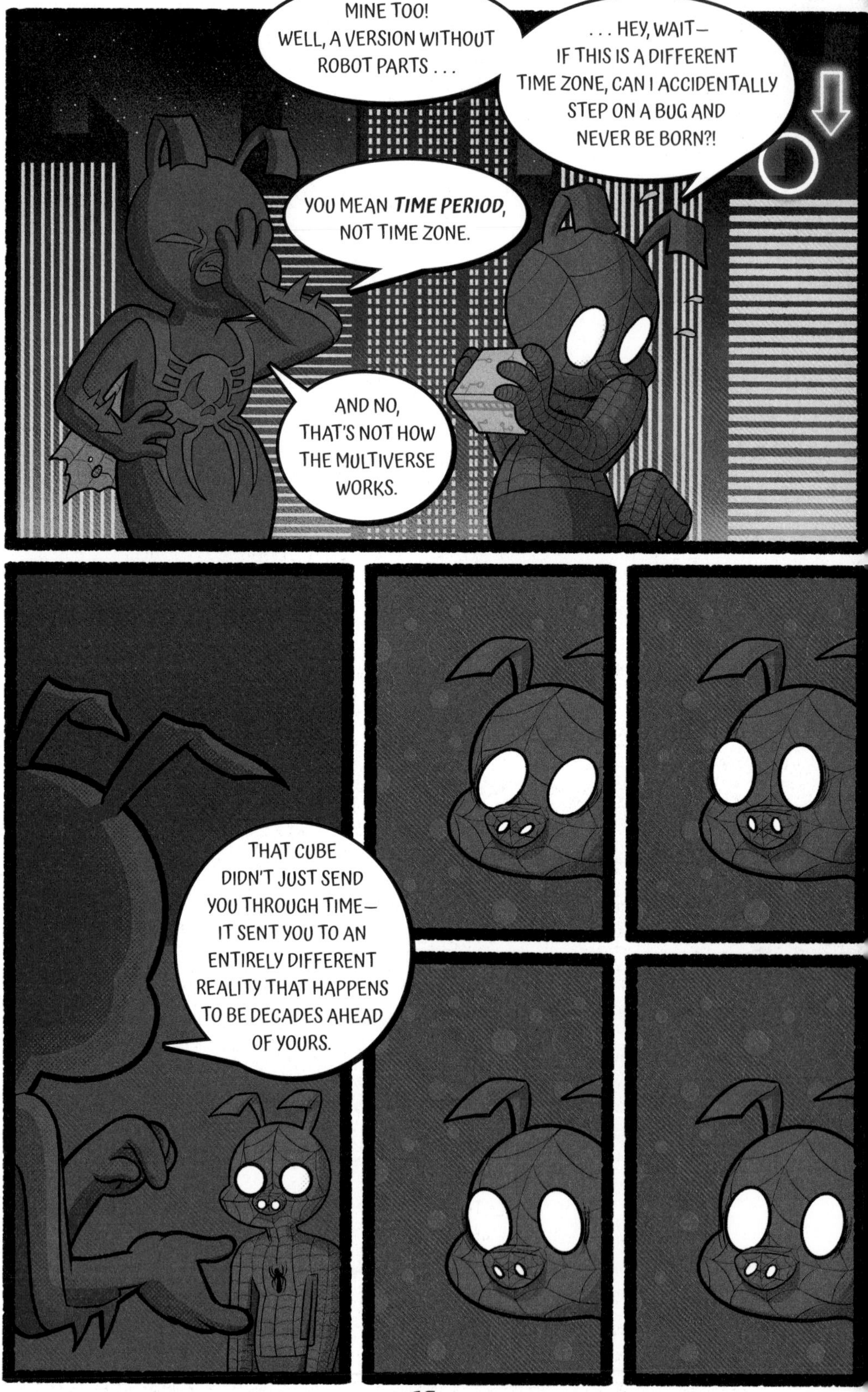
MINE TOO! WELL, A VERSION WITHOUT ROBOT PARTS . . .
. . . HEY, WAIT— IF THIS IS A DIFFERENT TIME ZONE, CAN I ACCIDENTALLY STEP ON A BUG AND NEVER BE BORN?!
YOU MEAN *TIME PERIOD*, NOT TIME ZONE.
AND NO, THAT'S NOT HOW THE MULTIVERSE WORKS.
THAT CUBE DIDN'T JUST SEND YOU THROUGH TIME— IT SENT YOU TO AN ENTIRELY DIFFERENT REALITY THAT HAPPENS TO BE DECADES AHEAD OF YOURS.

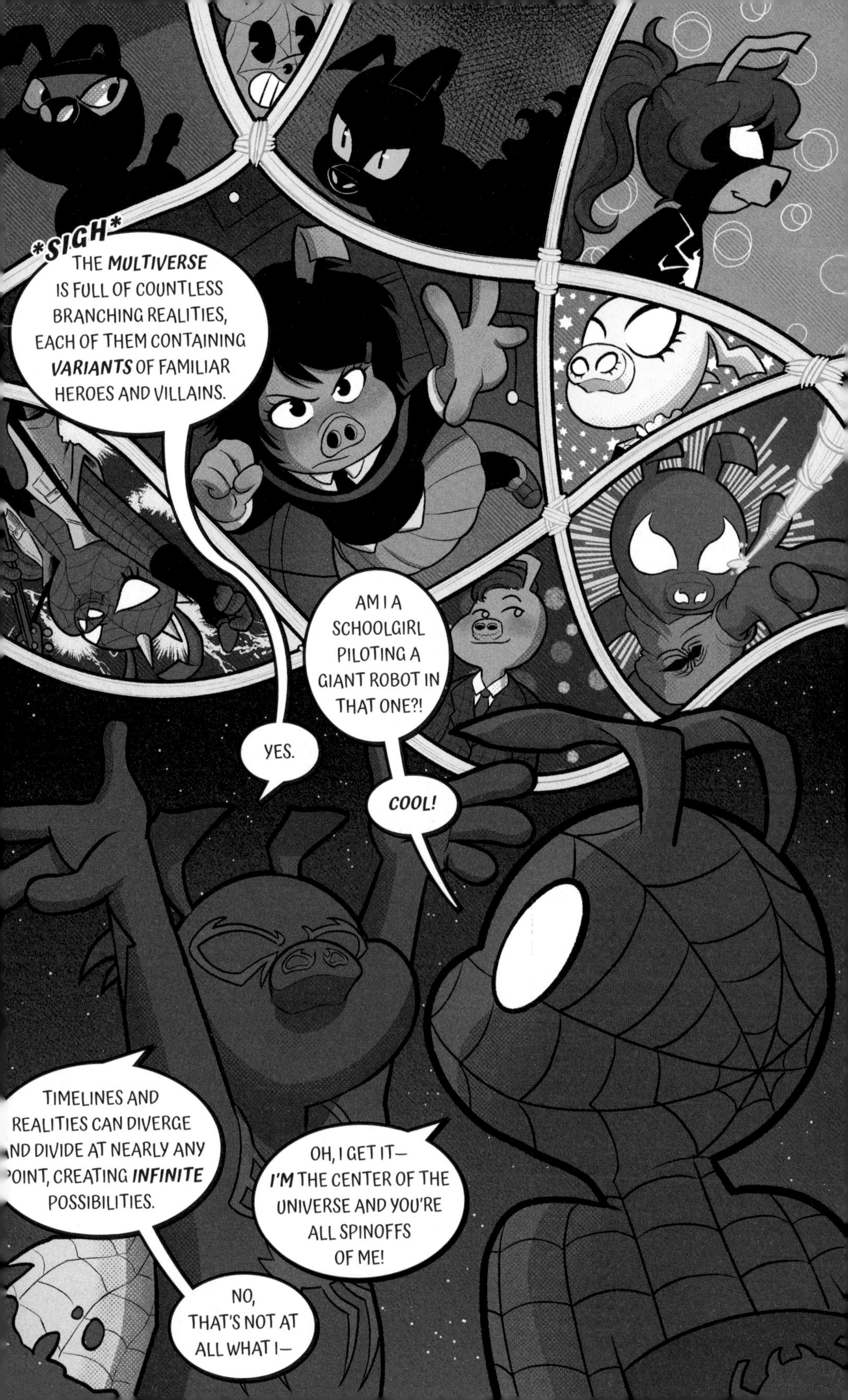
*SIGH*
THE MULTIVERSE IS FULL OF COUNTLESS BRANCHING REALITIES, EACH OF THEM CONTAINING VARIANTS OF FAMILIAR HEROES AND VILLAINS.
AM I A SCHOOLGIRL PILOTING A GIANT ROBOT IN THAT ONE?!
YES.
COOL!
TIMELINES AND REALITIES CAN DIVERGE AND DIVIDE AT NEARLY ANY POINT, CREATING INFINITE POSSIBILITIES.
OH, I GET IT— I'M THE CENTER OF THE UNIVERSE AND YOU'RE ALL SPINOFFS OF ME!
NO, THAT'S NOT AT ALL WHAT I—

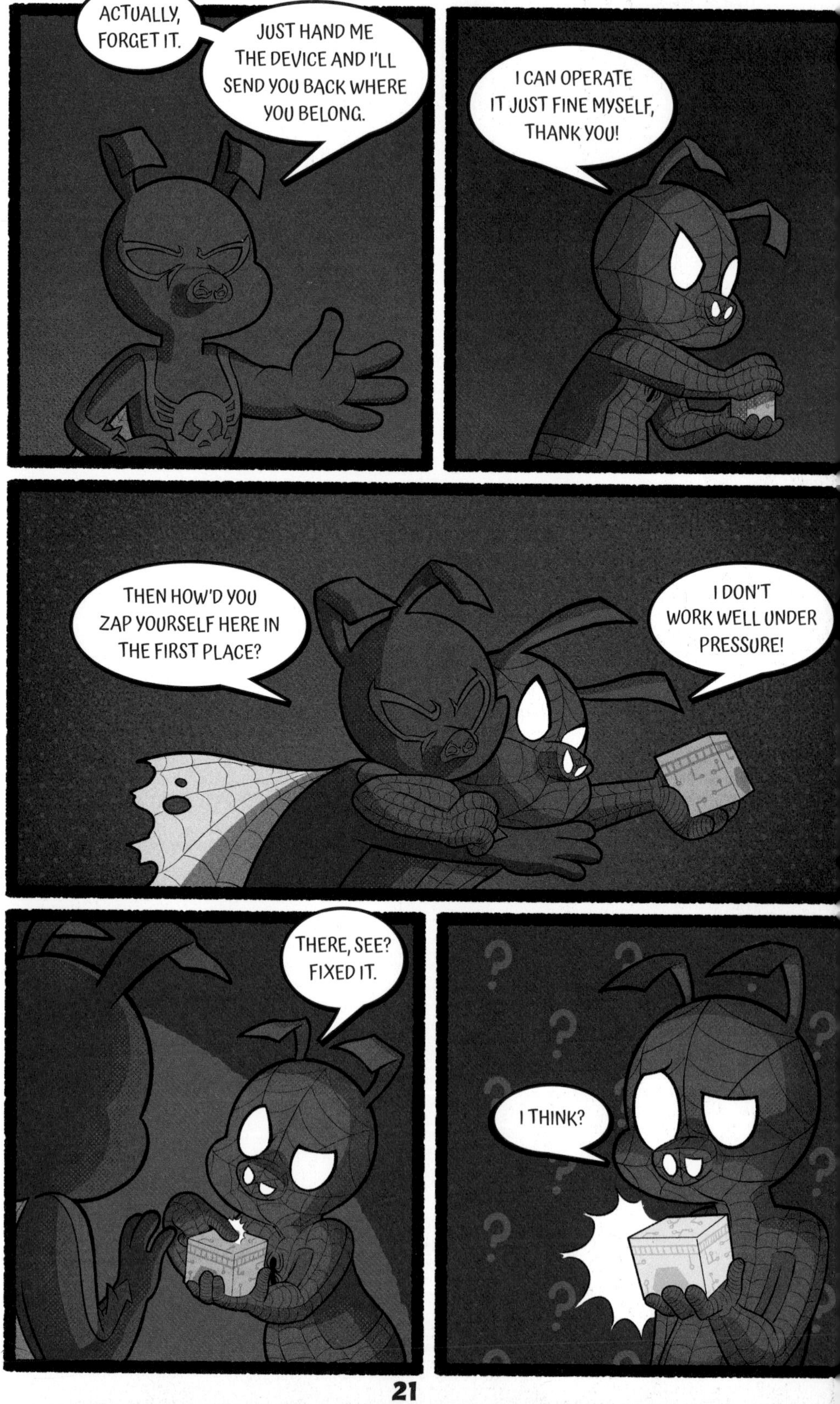
ACTUALLY, FORGET IT.
JUST HAND ME THE DEVICE AND I'LL SEND YOU BACK WHERE YOU BELONG.
I CAN OPERATE IT JUST FINE MYSELF, THANK YOU!
THEN HOW'D YOU ZAP YOURSELF HERE IN THE FIRST PLACE?
I DON'T WORK WELL UNDER PRESSURE!
THERE, SEE? FIXED IT.
I THINK?

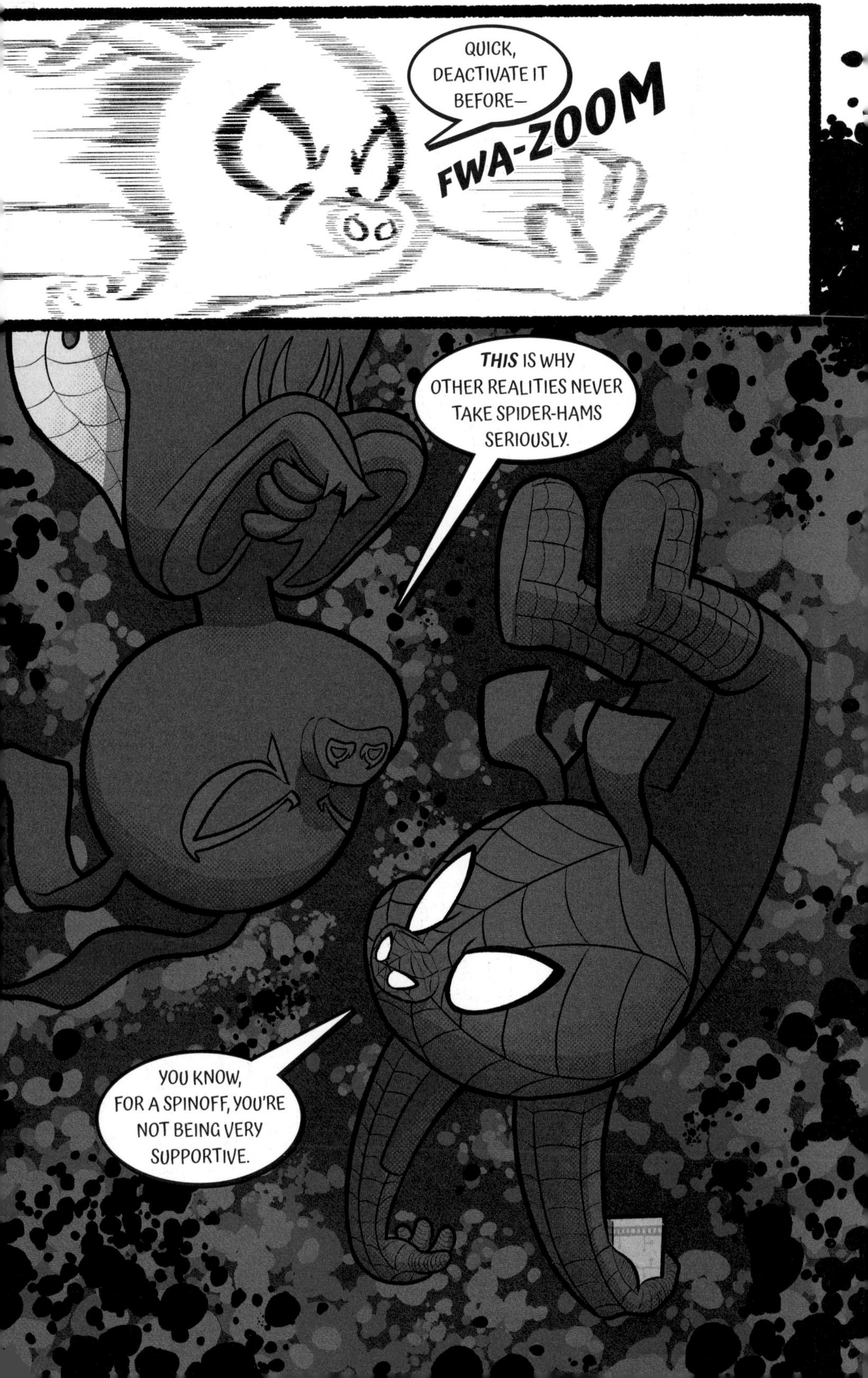
QUICK, DEACTIVATE IT BEFORE—
FWA-ZOOM
THIS IS WHY OTHER REALITIES NEVER TAKE SPIDER-HAMS SERIOUSLY.
YOU KNOW, FOR A SPINOFF, YOU'RE NOT BEING VERY SUPPORTIVE.

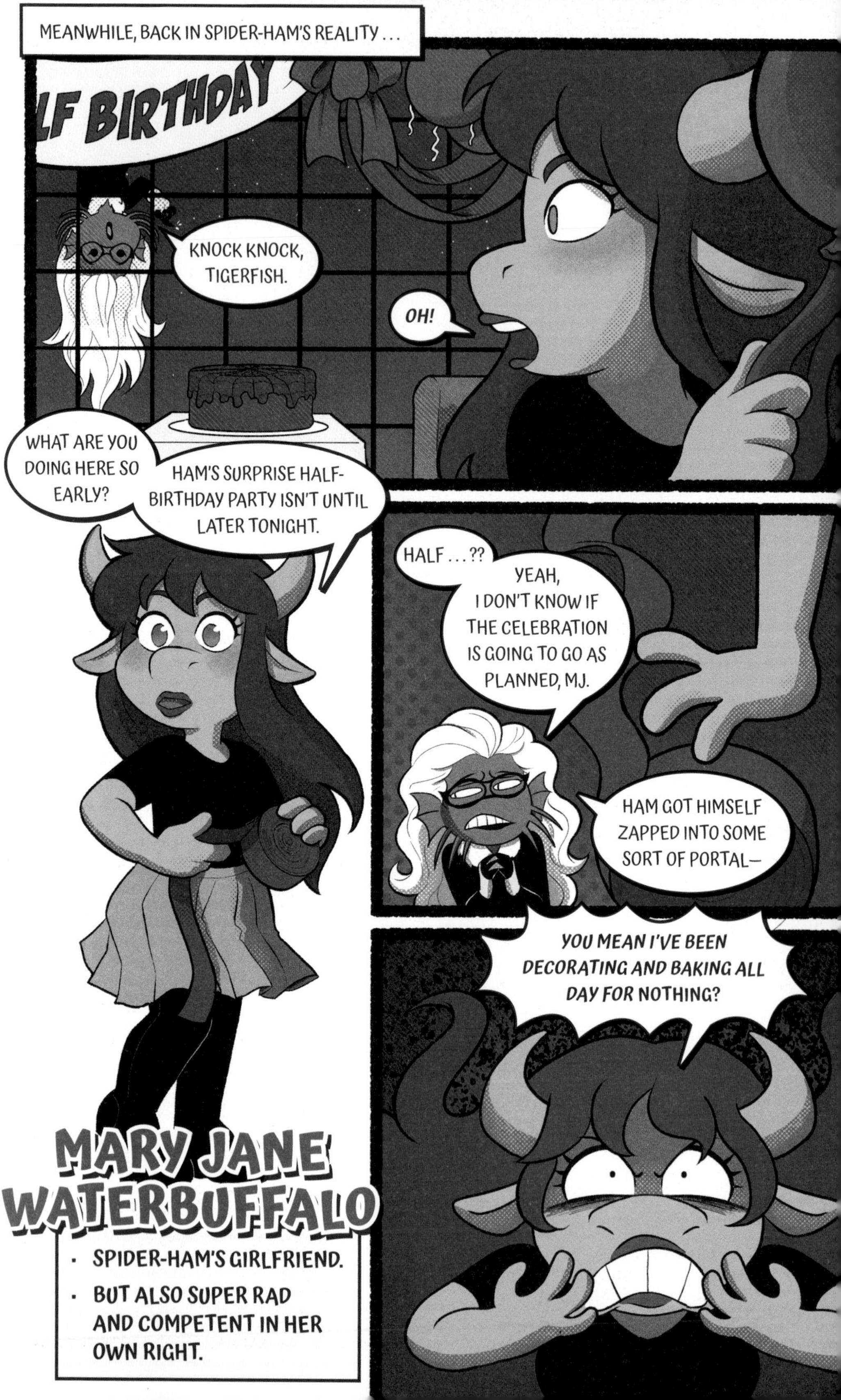
MEANWHILE, BACK IN SPIDER-HAM'S REALITY . . .
LF BIRTHDAY
KNOCK KNOCK, TIGERFISH.
OH!
WHAT ARE YOU DOING HERE SO EARLY?
HAM'S SURPRISE HALF-BIRTHDAY PARTY ISN'T UNTIL LATER TONIGHT.
MARY JANE WATERBUFFALO
• SPIDER-HAM'S GIRLFRIEND.
• BUT ALSO SUPER RAD AND COMPETENT IN HER OWN RIGHT.
HALF . . . ??
YEAH, I DON'T KNOW IF THE CELEBRATION IS GOING TO GO AS PLANNED, MJ.
HAM GOT HIMSELF ZAPPED INTO SOME SORT OF PORTAL—
YOU MEAN I'VE BEEN DECORATING AND BAKING ALL DAY FOR NOTHING?

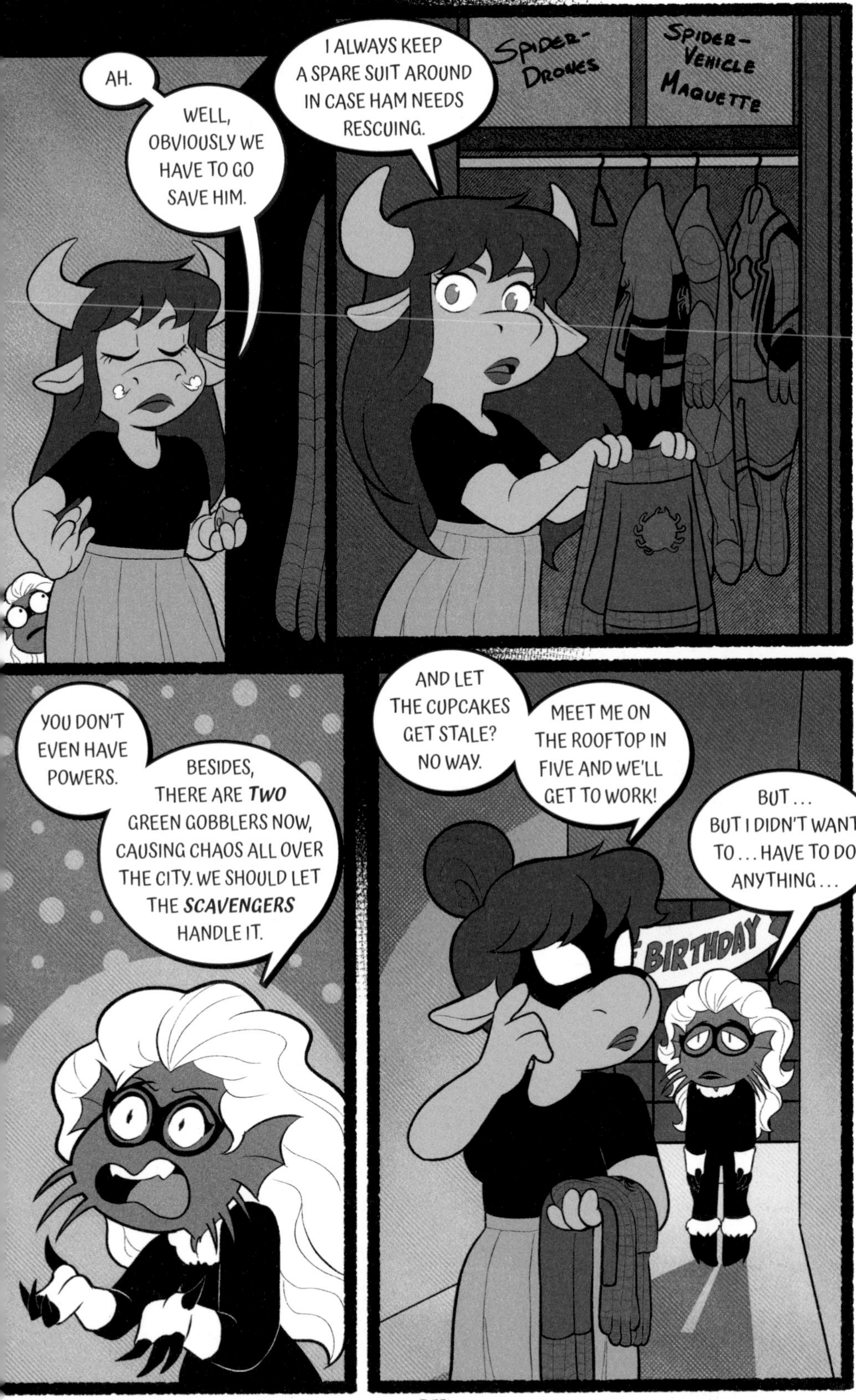
AH.
WELL, OBVIOUSLY WE HAVE TO GO SAVE HIM.
I ALWAYS KEEP A SPARE SUIT AROUND IN CASE HAM NEEDS RESCUING.
SPIDER-DRONES
SPIDER-VEHICLE MAQUETTE
YOU DON'T EVEN HAVE POWERS.
BESIDES, THERE ARE *TWO* GREEN GOBBLERS NOW, CAUSING CHAOS ALL OVER THE CITY. WE SHOULD LET THE ***SCAVENGERS*** HANDLE IT.
AND LET THE CUPCAKES GET STALE? NO WAY.
MEET ME ON THE ROOFTOP IN FIVE AND WE'LL GET TO WORK!
BUT . . . BUT I DIDN'T WANT TO . . . HAVE TO DO ANYTHING . . .
BIRTHDAY

# CHAPTER THREE:
# JURASSIC PORK!

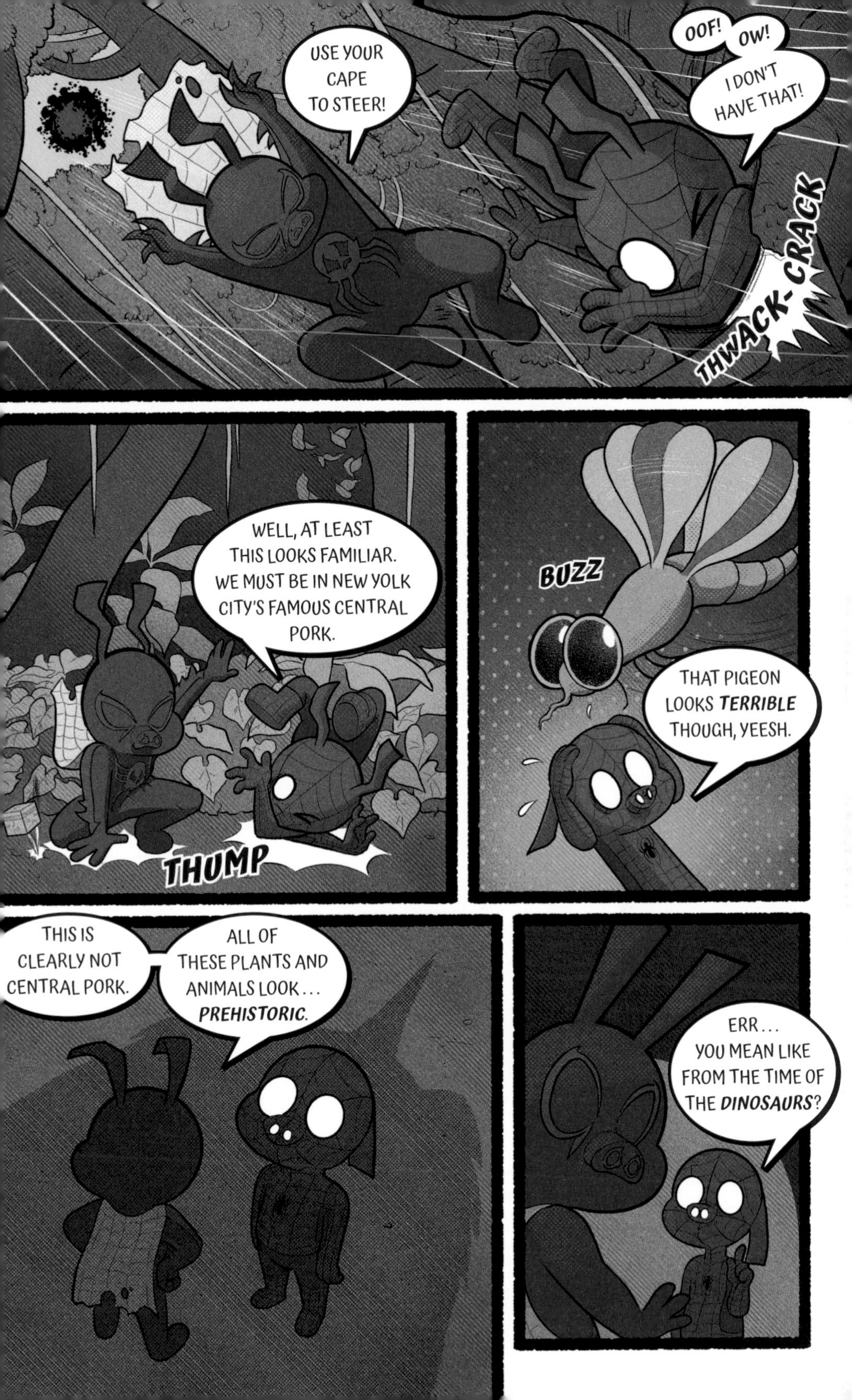
USE YOUR CAPE TO STEER!
OOF!
OW!
I DON'T HAVE THAT!
THWACK-CRACK
WELL, AT LEAST THIS LOOKS FAMILIAR. WE MUST BE IN NEW YOLK CITY'S FAMOUS CENTRAL PORK.
THUMP
BUZZ
THAT PIGEON LOOKS TERRIBLE THOUGH, YEESH.
THIS IS CLEARLY NOT CENTRAL PORK.
ALL OF THESE PLANTS AND ANIMALS LOOK . . . PREHISTORIC.
ERR . . . YOU MEAN LIKE FROM THE TIME OF THE DINOSAURS?

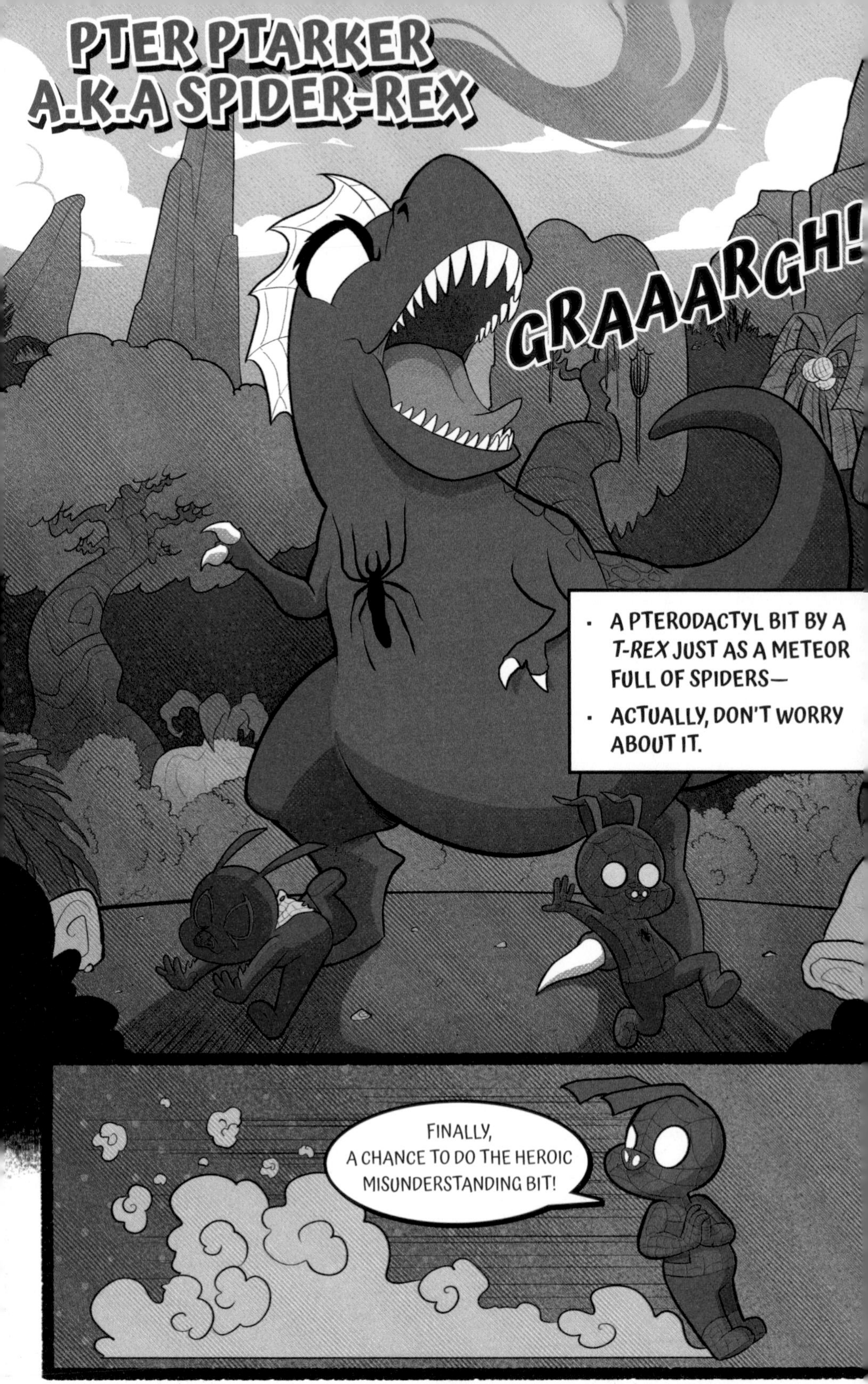
PTER PTARKER
A.K.A SPIDER-REX
GRAAARGH!
• A PTERODACTYL BIT BY A T-REX JUST AS A METEOR FULL OF SPIDERS—
• ACTUALLY, DON'T WORRY ABOUT IT.
FINALLY, A CHANCE TO DO THE HEROIC MISUNDERSTANDING BIT!

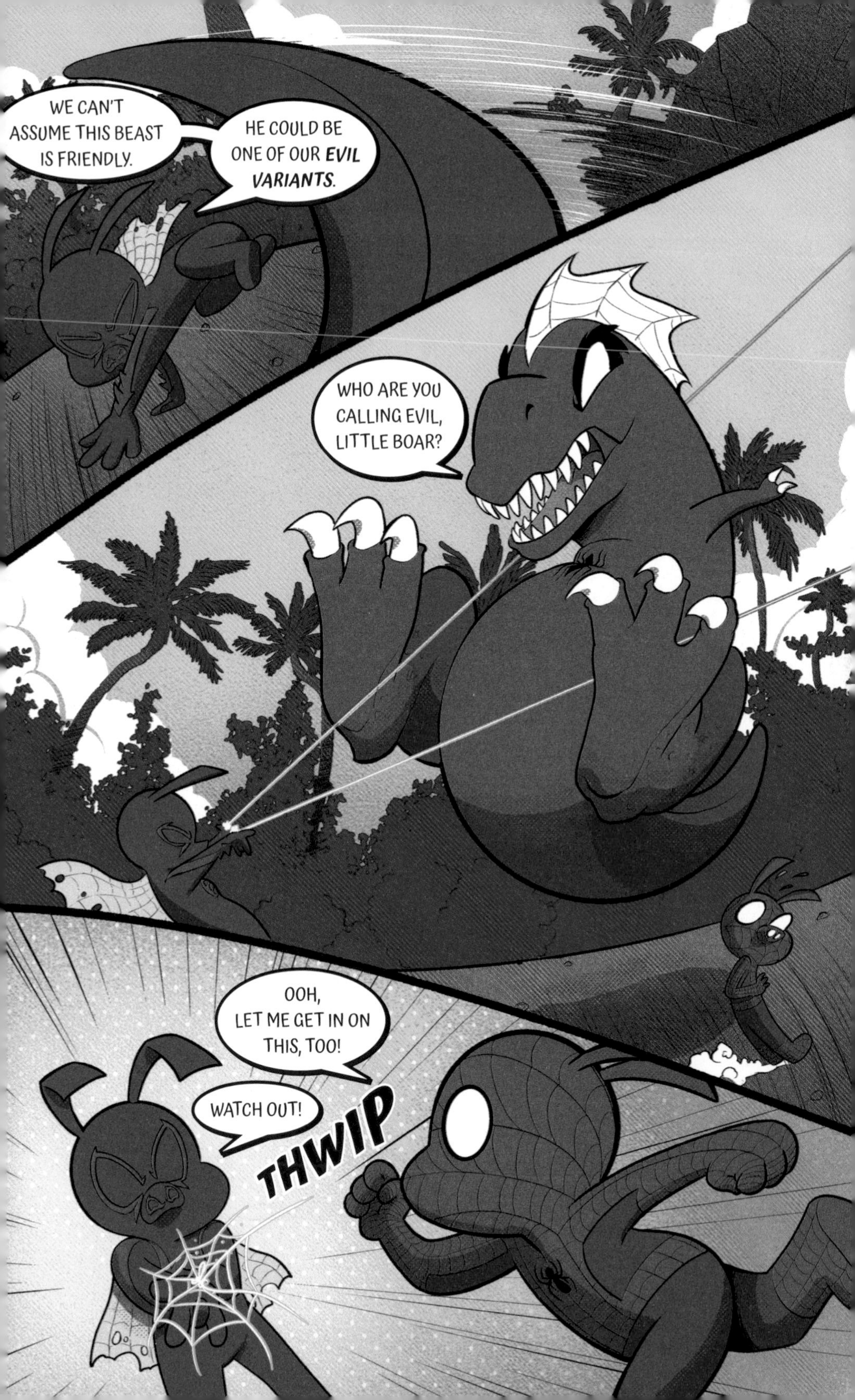
WE CAN'T ASSUME THIS BEAST IS FRIENDLY.
HE COULD BE ONE OF OUR **EVIL VARIANTS**.
WHO ARE YOU CALLING EVIL, LITTLE BOAR?
OOH, LET ME GET IN ON THIS, TOO!
WATCH OUT!
THWIP

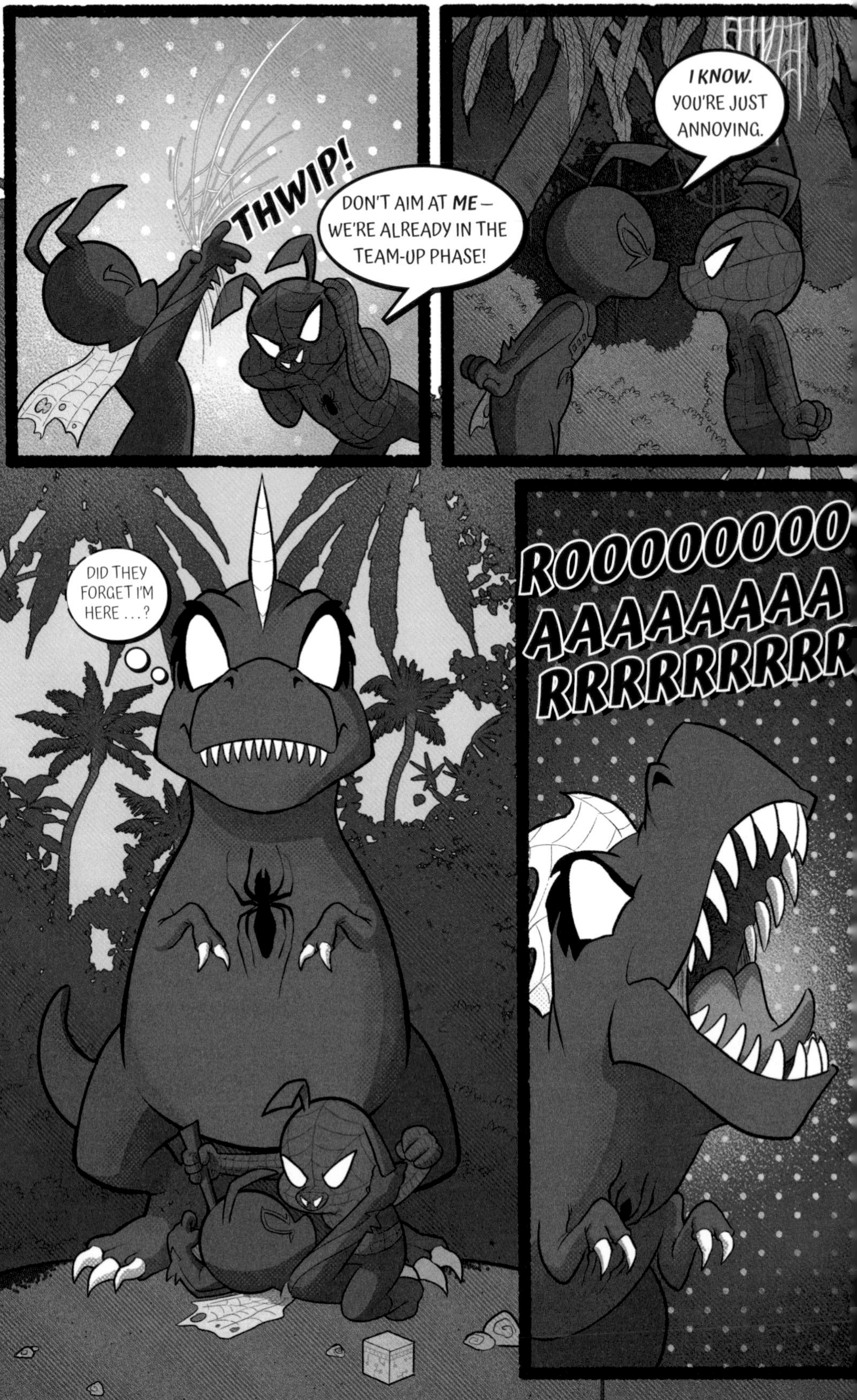
THWIP!
DON'T AIM AT ME — WE'RE ALREADY IN THE TEAM-UP PHASE!
I KNOW. YOU'RE JUST ANNOYING.
DID THEY FORGET I'M HERE . . . ?
ROOOOOOOOO AAAAAAAAA RRRRRRRRR

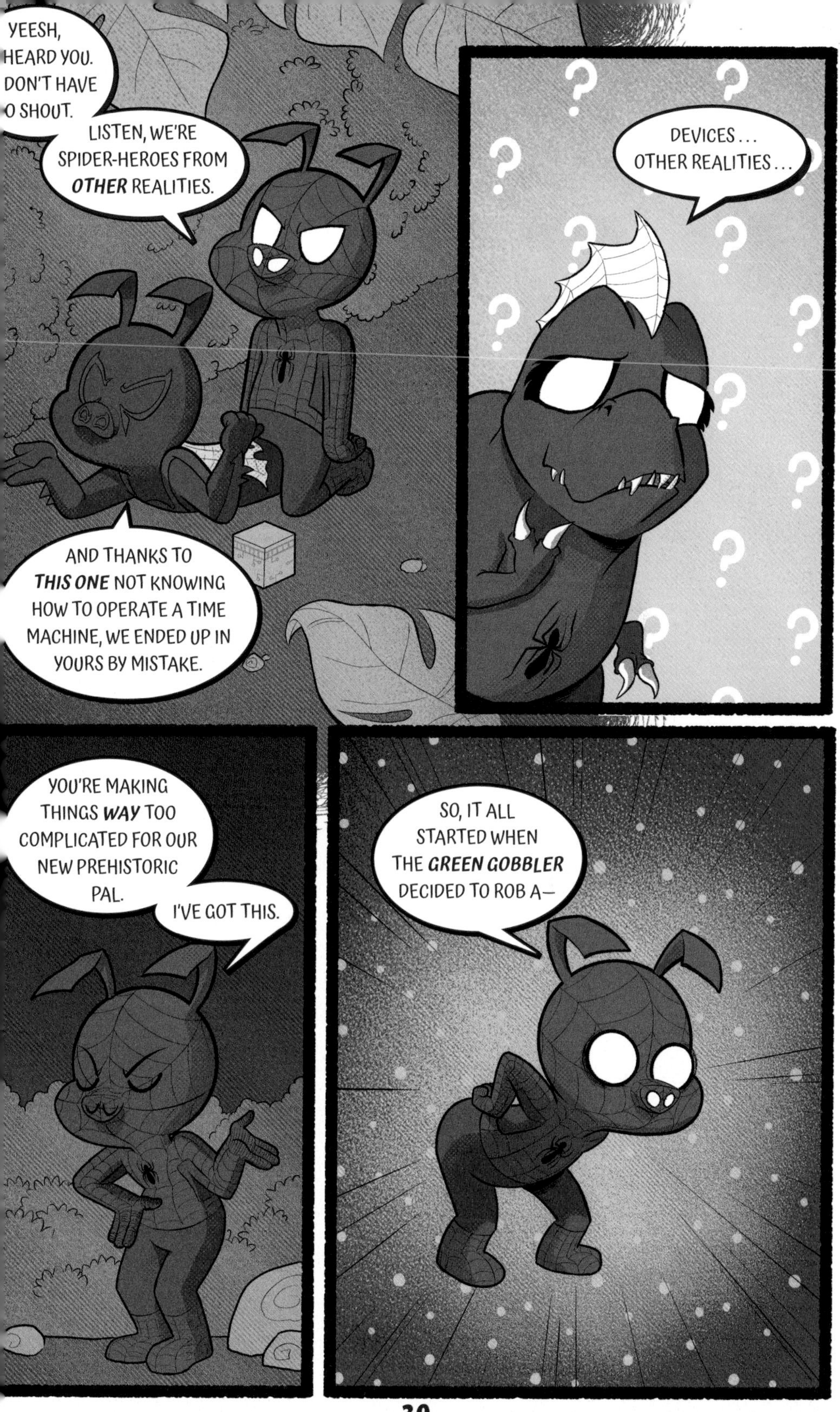
YEESH, HEARD YOU. DON'T HAVE O SHOUT.
LISTEN, WE'RE SPIDER-HEROES FROM **OTHER** REALITIES.
AND THANKS TO **THIS ONE** NOT KNOWING HOW TO OPERATE A TIME MACHINE, WE ENDED UP IN YOURS BY MISTAKE.
DEVICES . . . OTHER REALITIES . . .
YOU'RE MAKING THINGS **WAY** TOO COMPLICATED FOR OUR NEW PREHISTORIC PAL.
I'VE GOT THIS.
SO, IT ALL STARTED WHEN THE **GREEN GOBBLER** DECIDED TO ROB A—

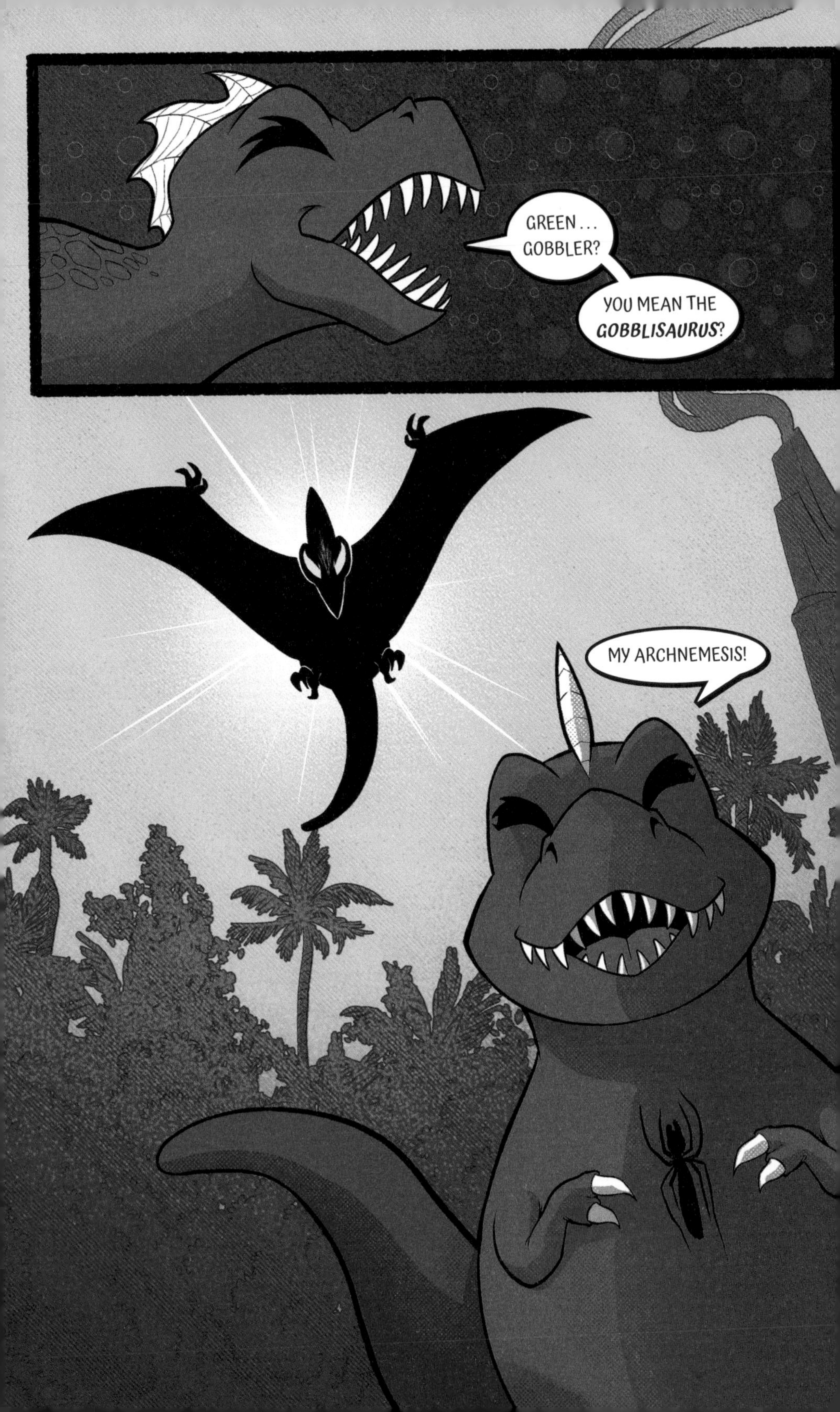
GREEN . . . GOBBLER?
YOU MEAN THE GOBBLISAURUS?
MY ARCHNEMESIS!

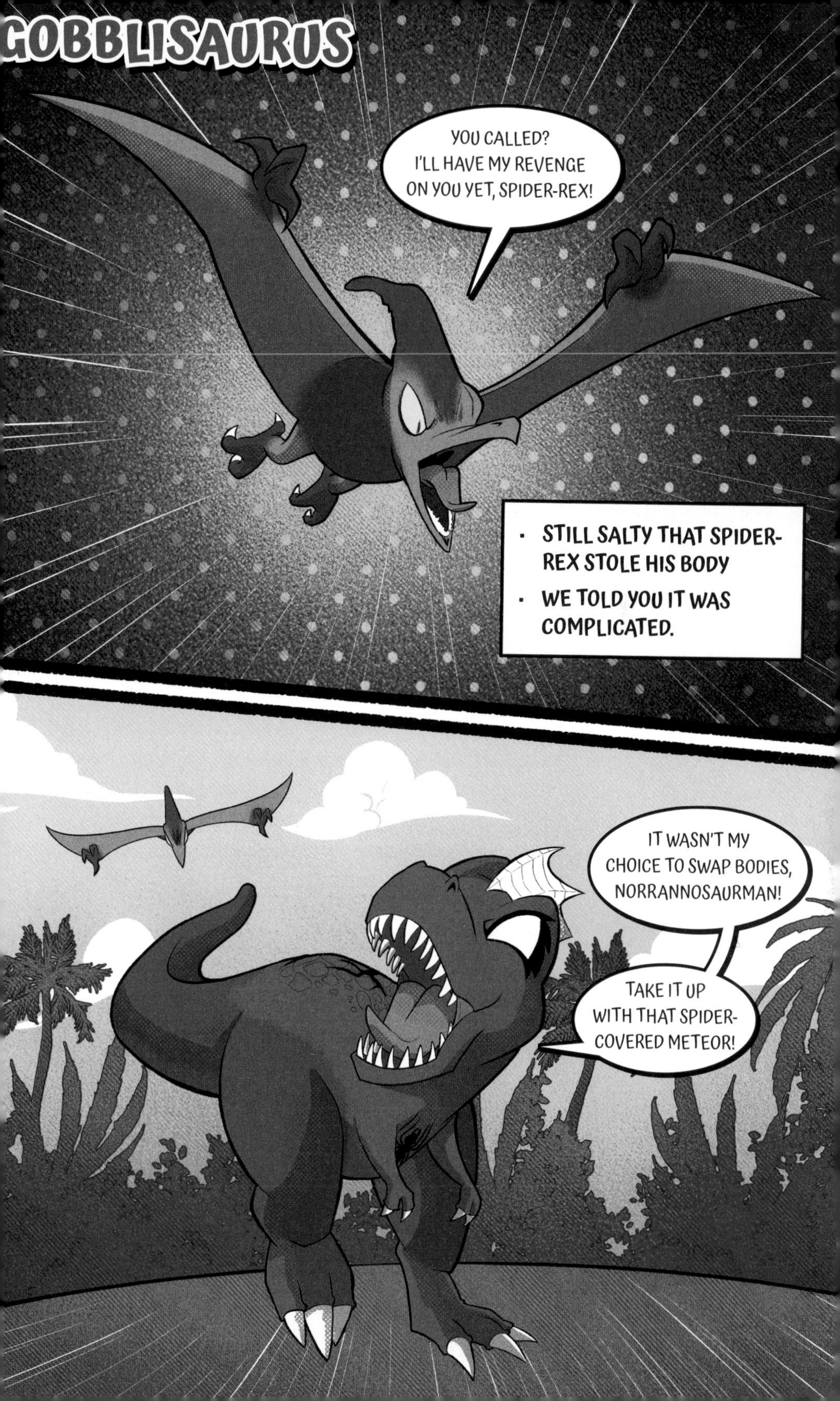
GOBBLISAURUS
YOU CALLED? I'LL HAVE MY REVENGE ON YOU YET, SPIDER-REX!
• STILL SALTY THAT SPIDER-REX STOLE HIS BODY
• WE TOLD YOU IT WAS COMPLICATED.
IT WASN'T MY CHOICE TO SWAP BODIES, NORRANNOSAURMAN!
TAKE IT UP WITH THAT SPIDER-COVERED METEOR!

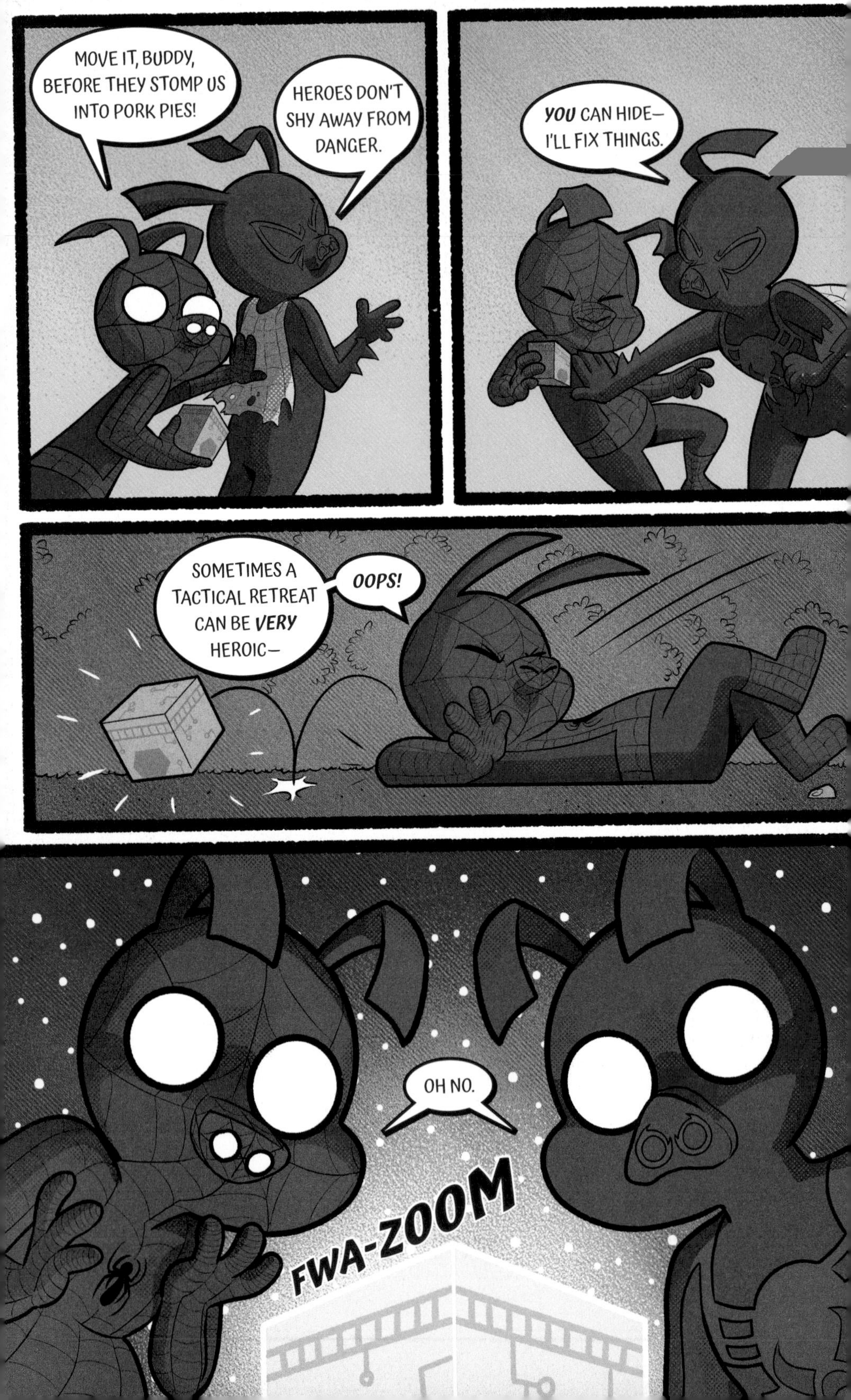
MOVE IT, BUDDY, BEFORE THEY STOMP US INTO PORK PIES!
HEROES DON'T SHY AWAY FROM DANGER.
YOU CAN HIDE— I'LL FIX THINGS.
SOMETIMES A TACTICAL RETREAT CAN BE VERY HEROIC—
OOPS!
OH NO.
FWA-ZOOM

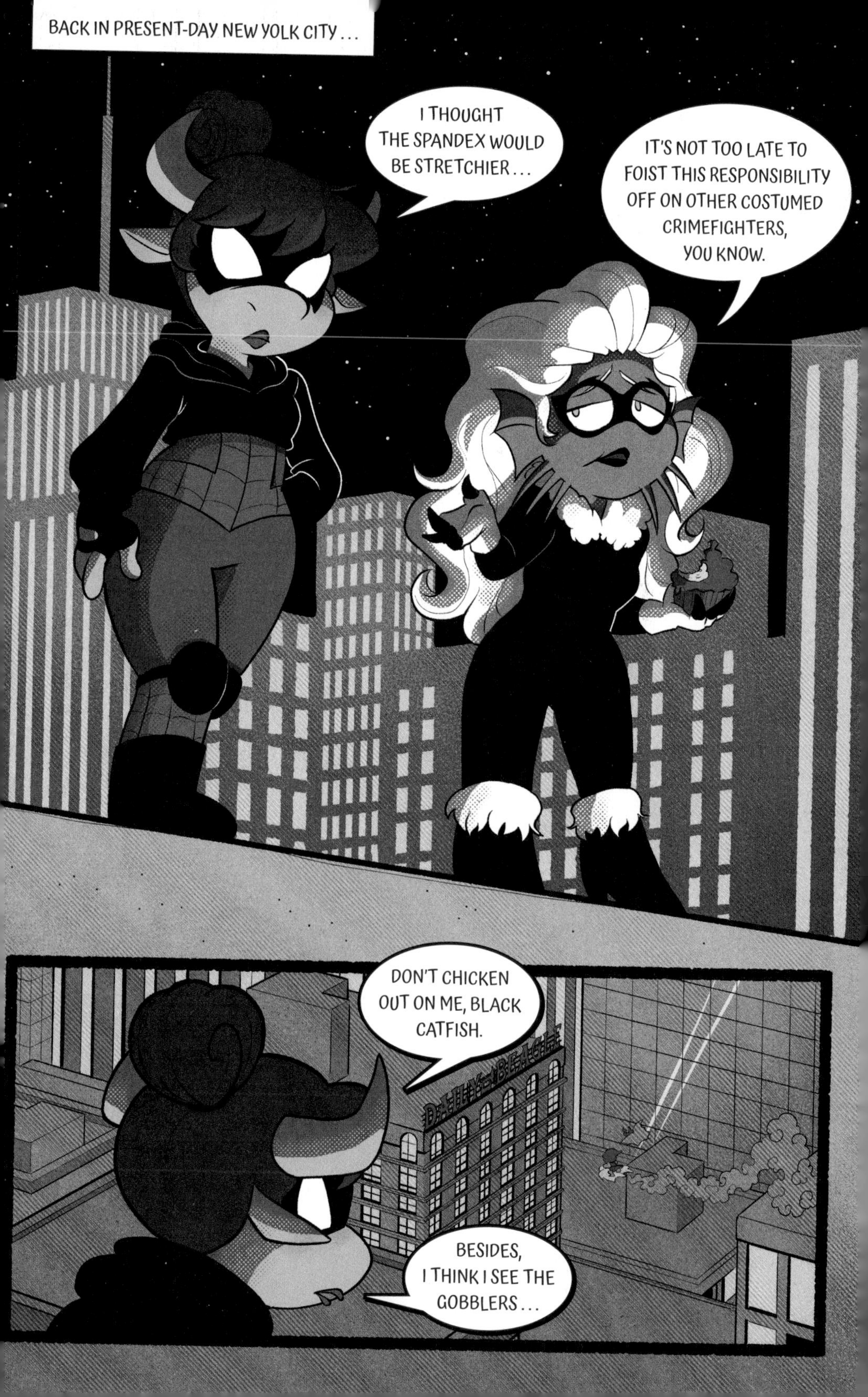
BACK IN PRESENT-DAY NEW YOLK CITY . . .
I THOUGHT THE SPANDEX WOULD BE STRETCHIER . . .
IT'S NOT TOO LATE TO FOIST THIS RESPONSIBILITY OFF ON OTHER COSTUMED CRIMEFIGHTERS, YOU KNOW.
DON'T CHICKEN OUT ON ME, BLACK CATFISH.
BESIDES, I THINK I SEE THE GOBBLERS . . .

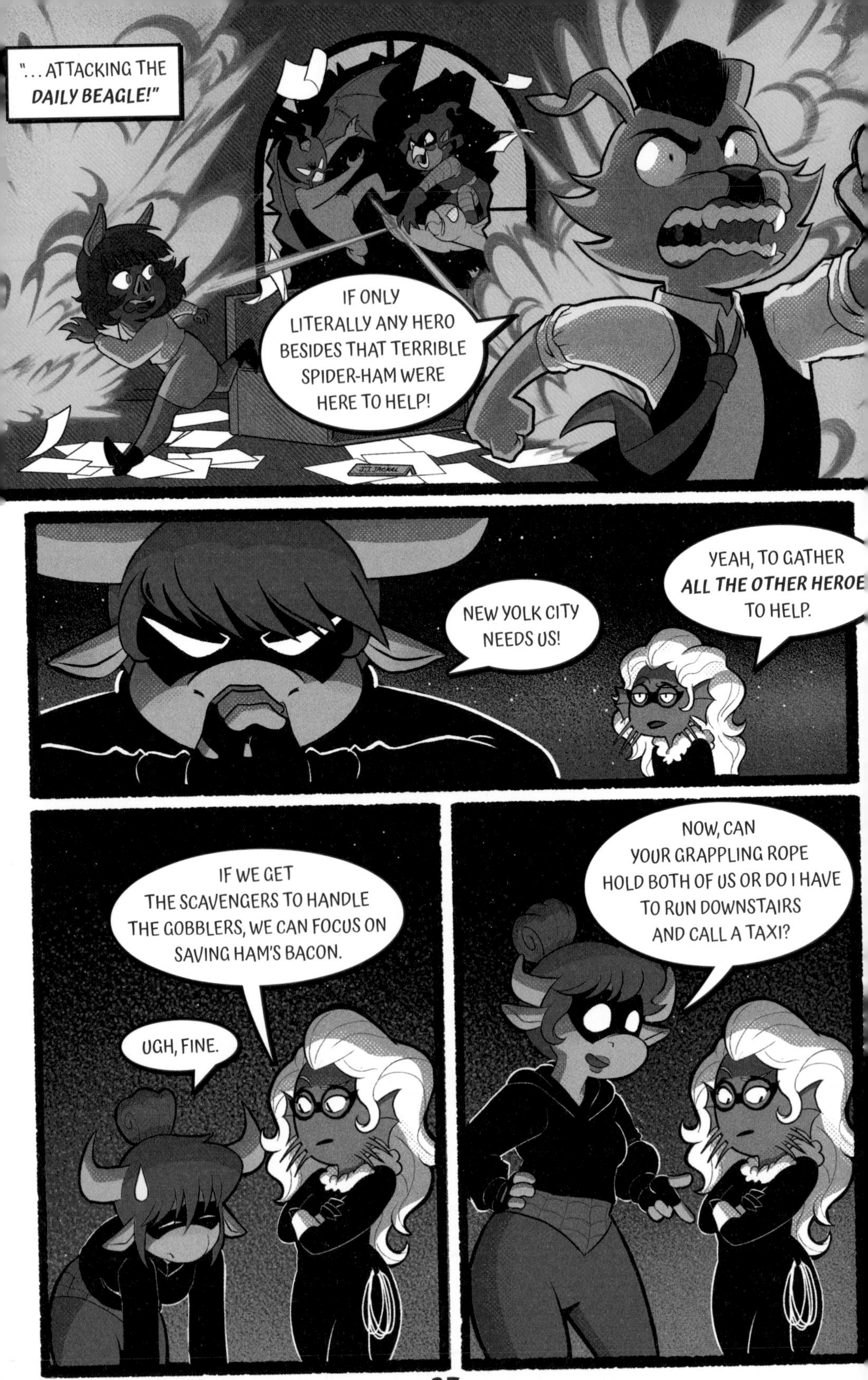
"...ATTACKING THE DAILY BEAGLE!"
IF ONLY LITERALLY ANY HERO BESIDES THAT TERRIBLE SPIDER-HAM WERE HERE TO HELP!
NEW YOLK CITY NEEDS US!
YEAH, TO GATHER ALL THE OTHER HEROE TO HELP.
IF WE GET THE SCAVENGERS TO HANDLE THE GOBBLERS, WE CAN FOCUS ON SAVING HAM'S BACON.
UGH, FINE.
NOW, CAN YOUR GRAPPLING ROPE HOLD BOTH OF US OR DO I HAVE TO RUN DOWNSTAIRS AND CALL A TAXI?

# CHAPTER FOUR:

# MULTIVERSE OF HAMNESS!

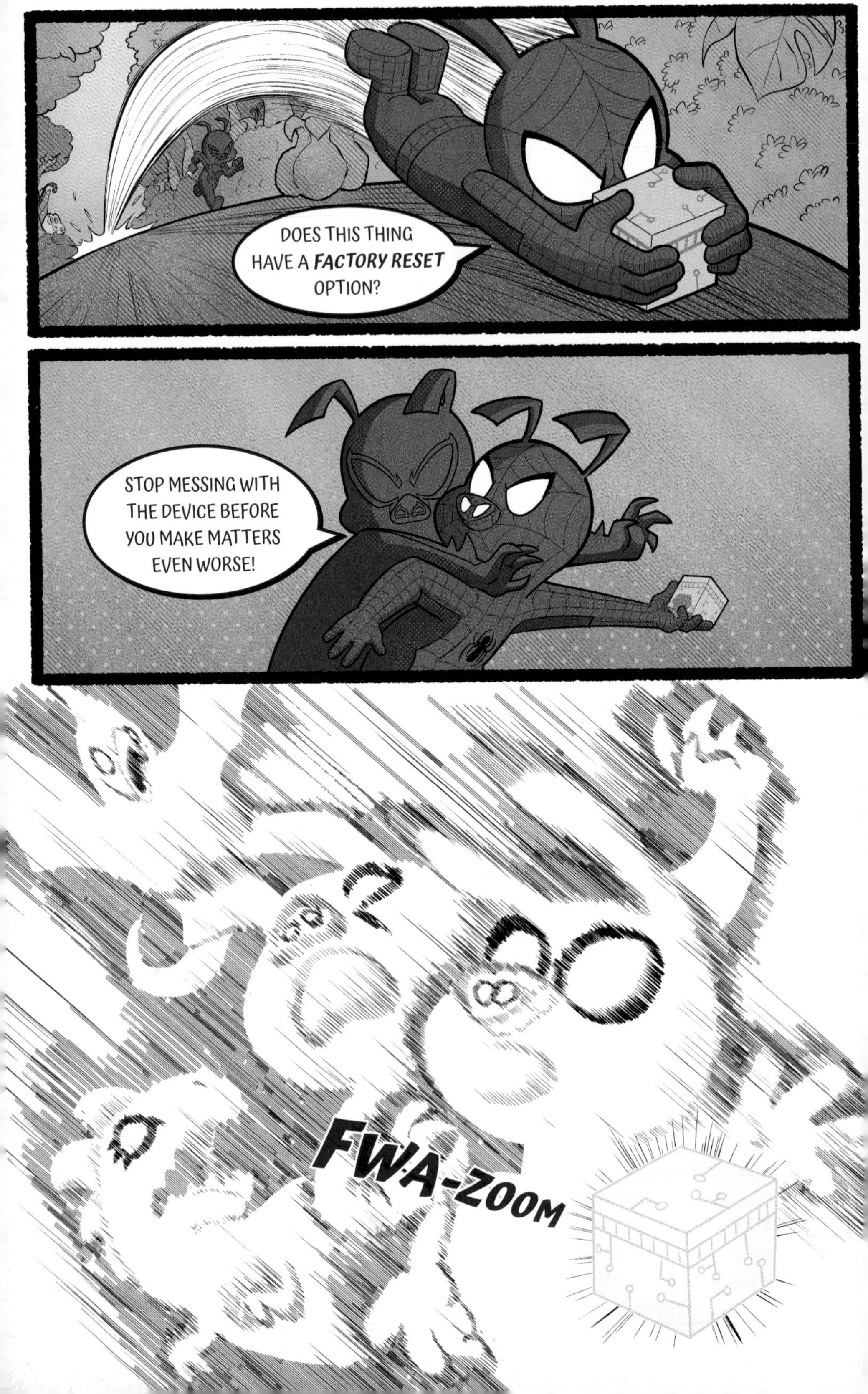
DOES THIS THING HAVE A FACTORY RESET OPTION?
STOP MESSING WITH THE DEVICE BEFORE YOU MAKE MATTERS EVEN WORSE!
FWA-ZOOM

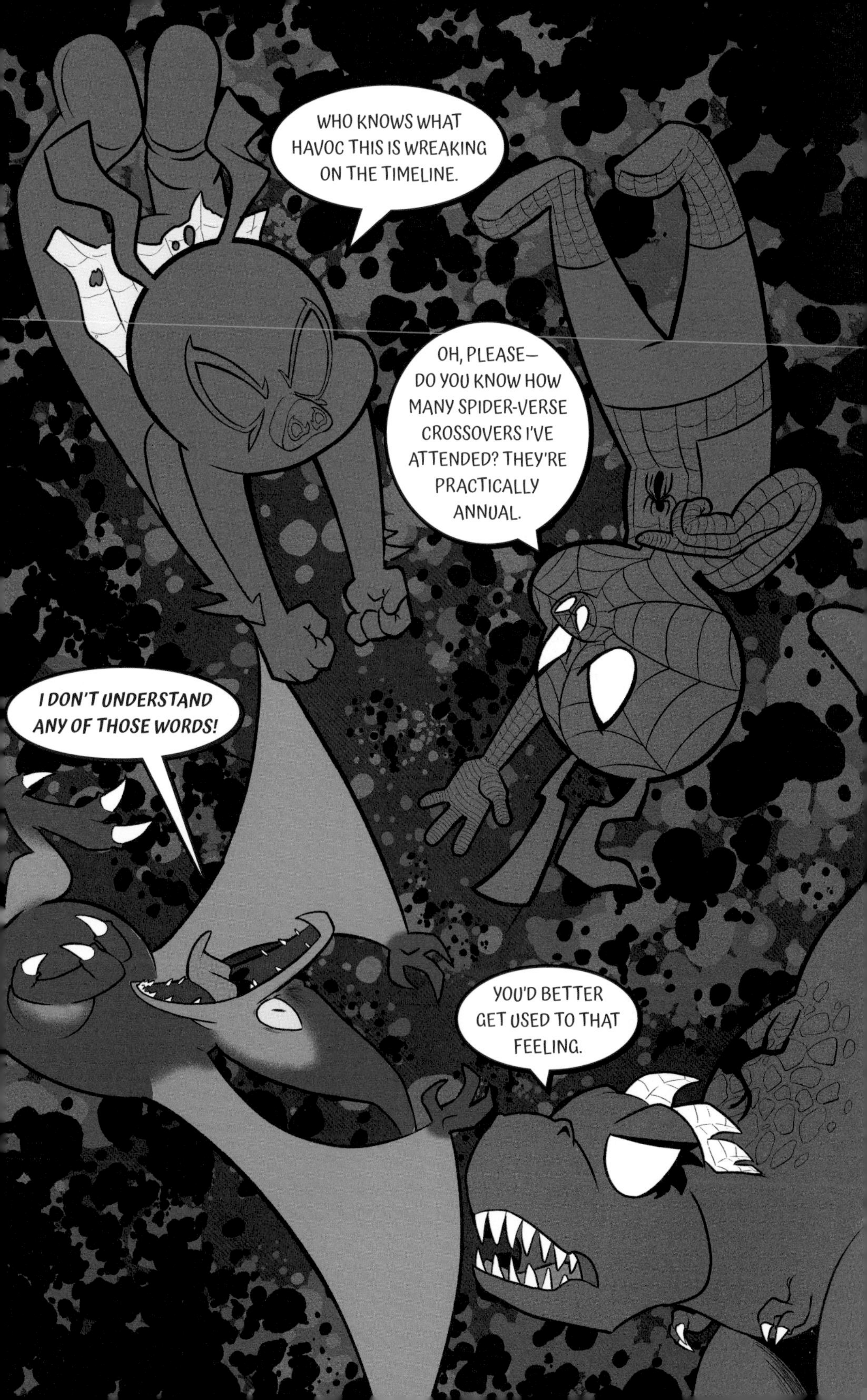
WHO KNOWS WHAT HAVOC THIS IS WREAKING ON THE TIMELINE.
OH, PLEASE— DO YOU KNOW HOW MANY SPIDER-VERSE CROSSOVERS I'VE ATTENDED? THEY'RE PRACTICALLY ANNUAL.
I DON'T UNDERSTAND ANY OF THOSE WORDS!
YOU'D BETTER GET USED TO THAT FEELING.

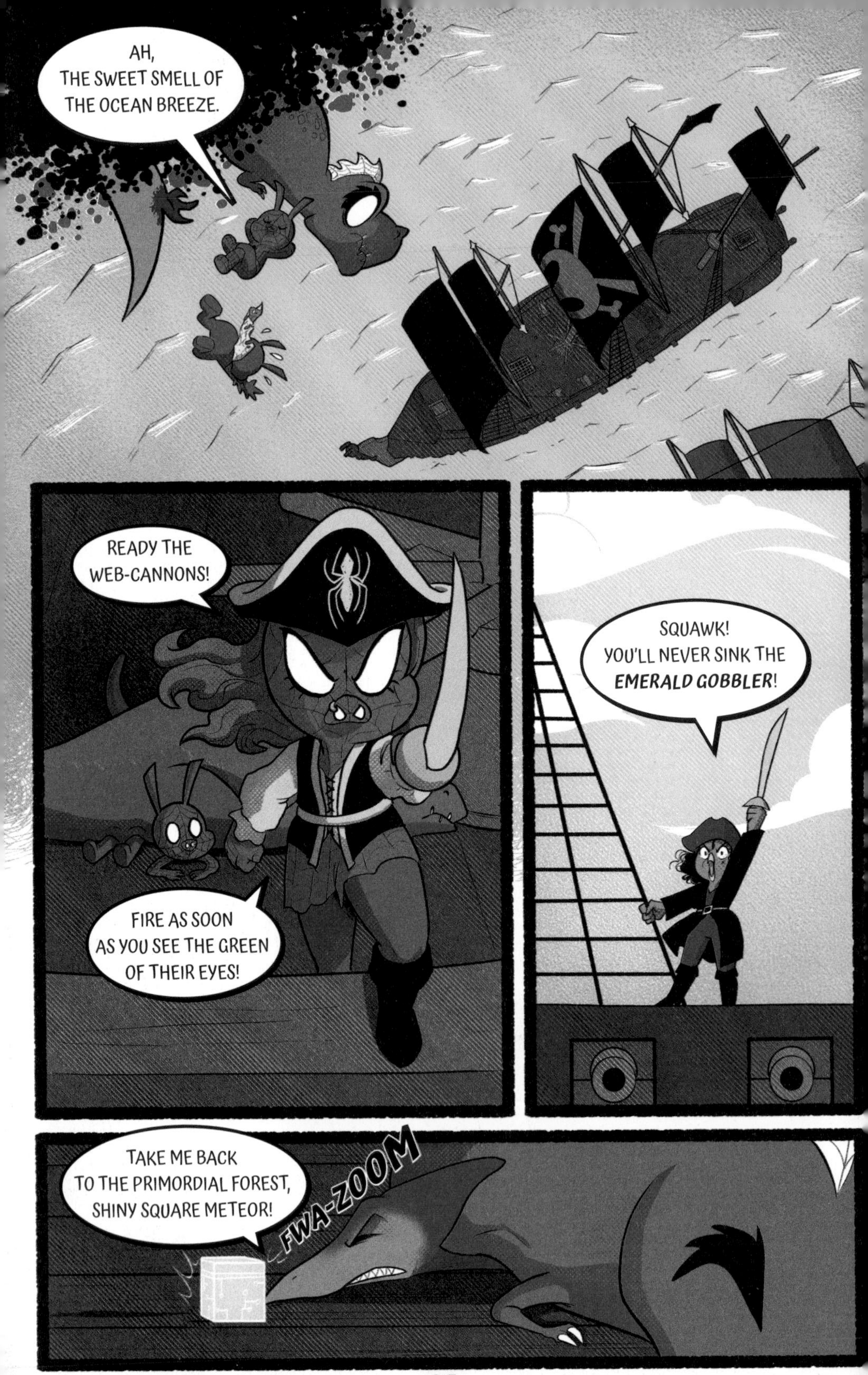
AH, THE SWEET SMELL OF THE OCEAN BREEZE.
READY THE WEB-CANNONS!
FIRE AS SOON AS YOU SEE THE GREEN OF THEIR EYES!
SQUAWK! YOU'LL NEVER SINK THE *EMERALD GOBBLER*!
TAKE ME BACK TO THE PRIMORDIAL FOREST, SHINY SQUARE METEOR!
FWA-ZOOM

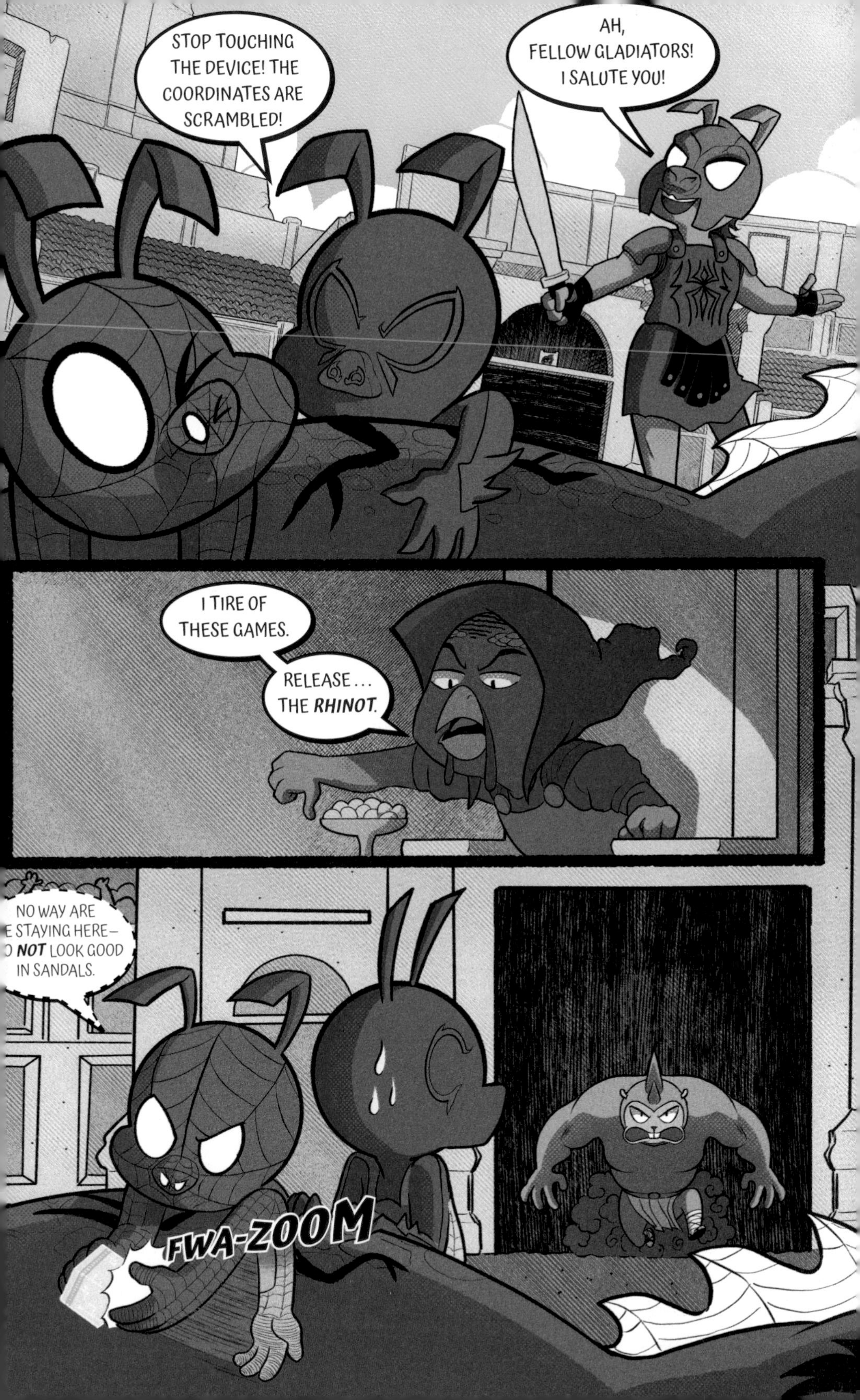
STOP TOUCHING THE DEVICE! THE COORDINATES ARE SCRAMBLED!
AH, FELLOW GLADIATORS! I SALUTE YOU!
I TIRE OF THESE GAMES.
RELEASE . . . THE *RHINOT*.
NO WAY ARE
E STAYING HERE—
O **NOT** LOOK GOOD
IN SANDALS.
FWA-ZOOM

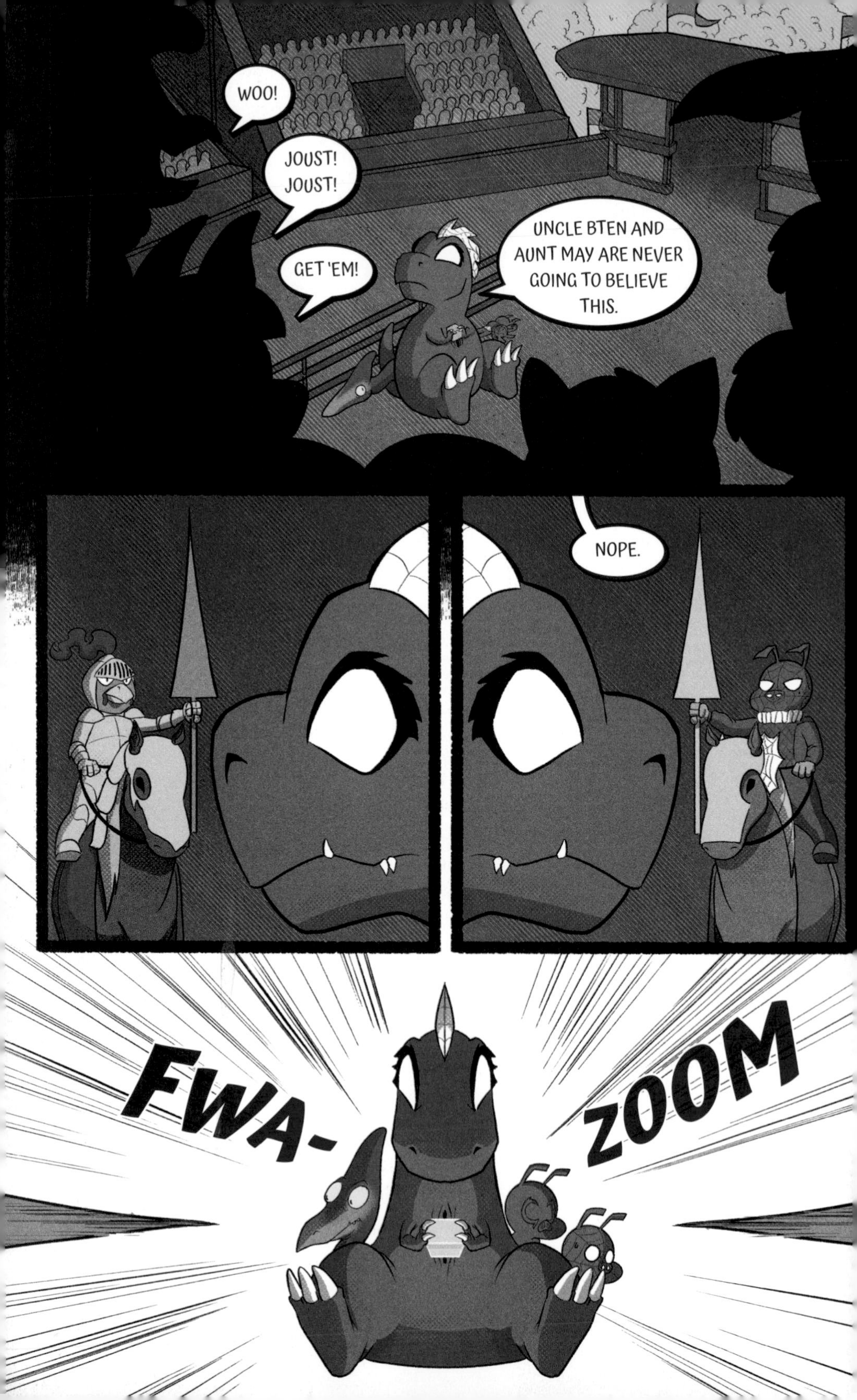
WOO!
JOUST! JOUST!
GET 'EM!
UNCLE BTEN AND AUNT MAY ARE NEVER GOING TO BELIEVE THIS.
NOPE.
FWA-ZOOM

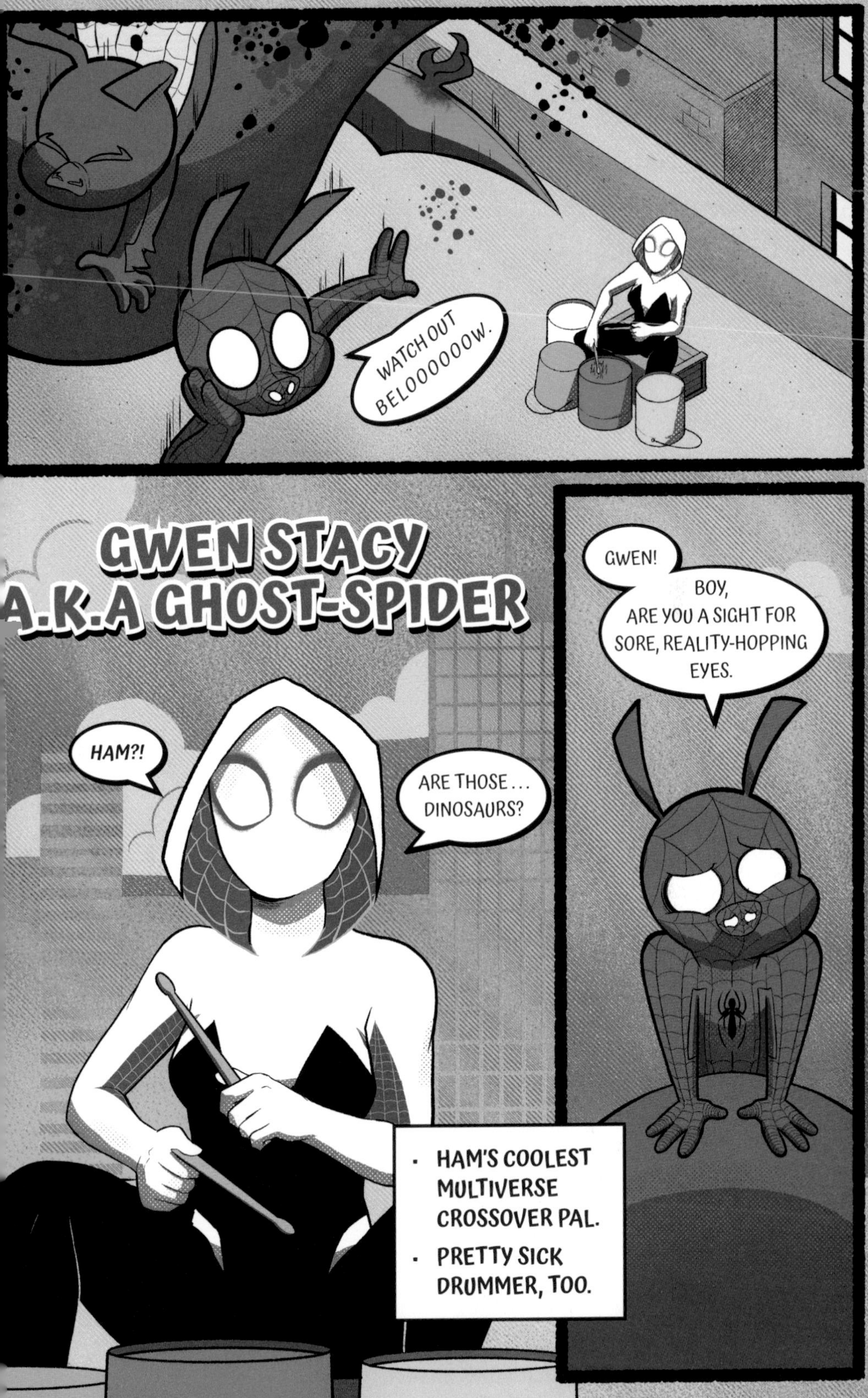

WATCH OUT BELOOOOOOW.
GWEN STACY A.K.A GHOST-SPIDER
HAM?!
ARE THOSE . . . DINOSAURS?
GWEN!
BOY, ARE YOU A SIGHT FOR SORE, REALITY-HOPPING EYES.
• HAM'S COOLEST MULTIVERSE CROSSOVER PAL.
• PRETTY SICK DRUMMER, TOO.

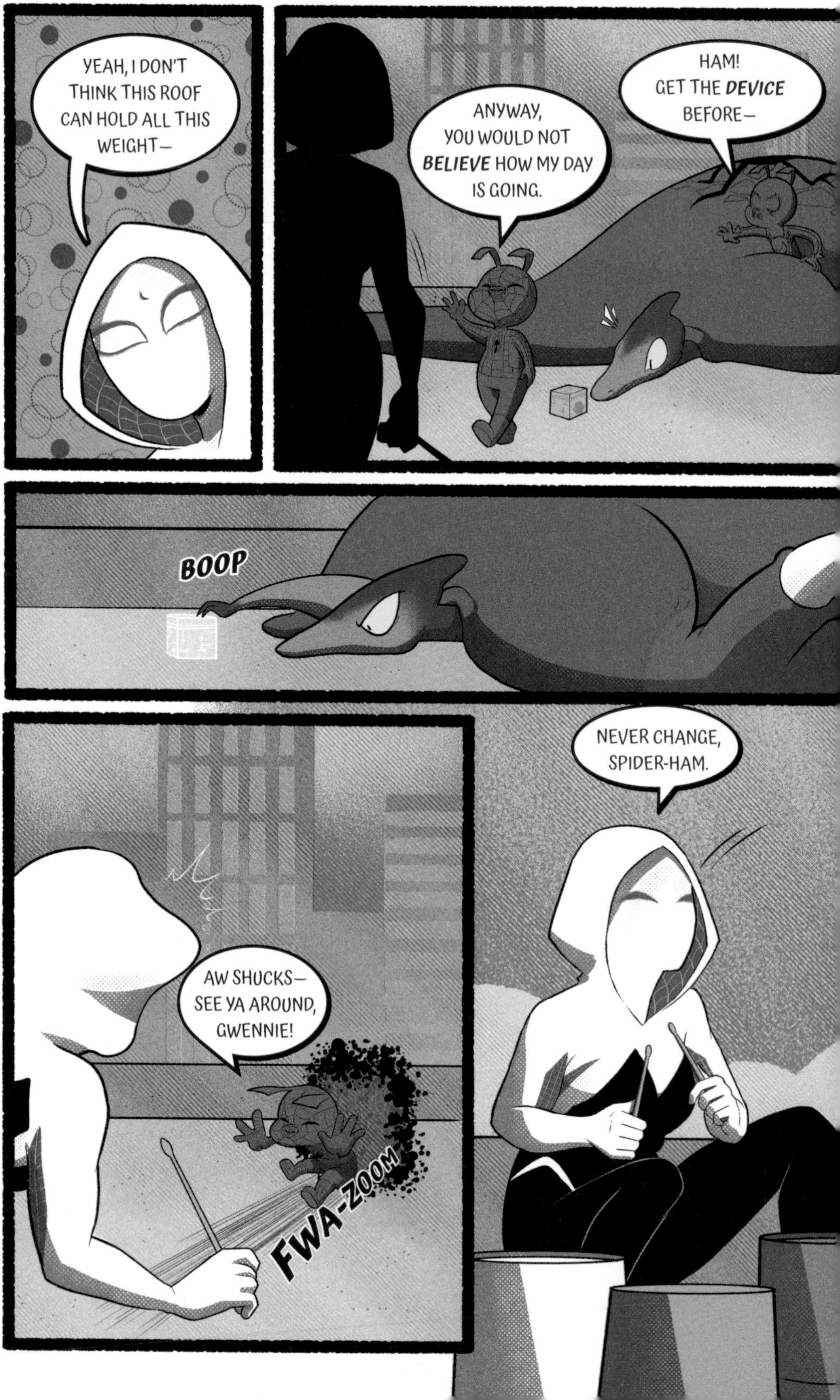
YEAH, I DON'T THINK THIS ROOF CAN HOLD ALL THIS WEIGHT—
ANYWAY, YOU WOULD NOT BELIEVE HOW MY DAY IS GOING.
HAM! GET THE DEVICE BEFORE—
BOOP
NEVER CHANGE, SPIDER-HAM.
AW SHUCKS— SEE YA AROUND, GWENNIE!
FWA-ZOOM

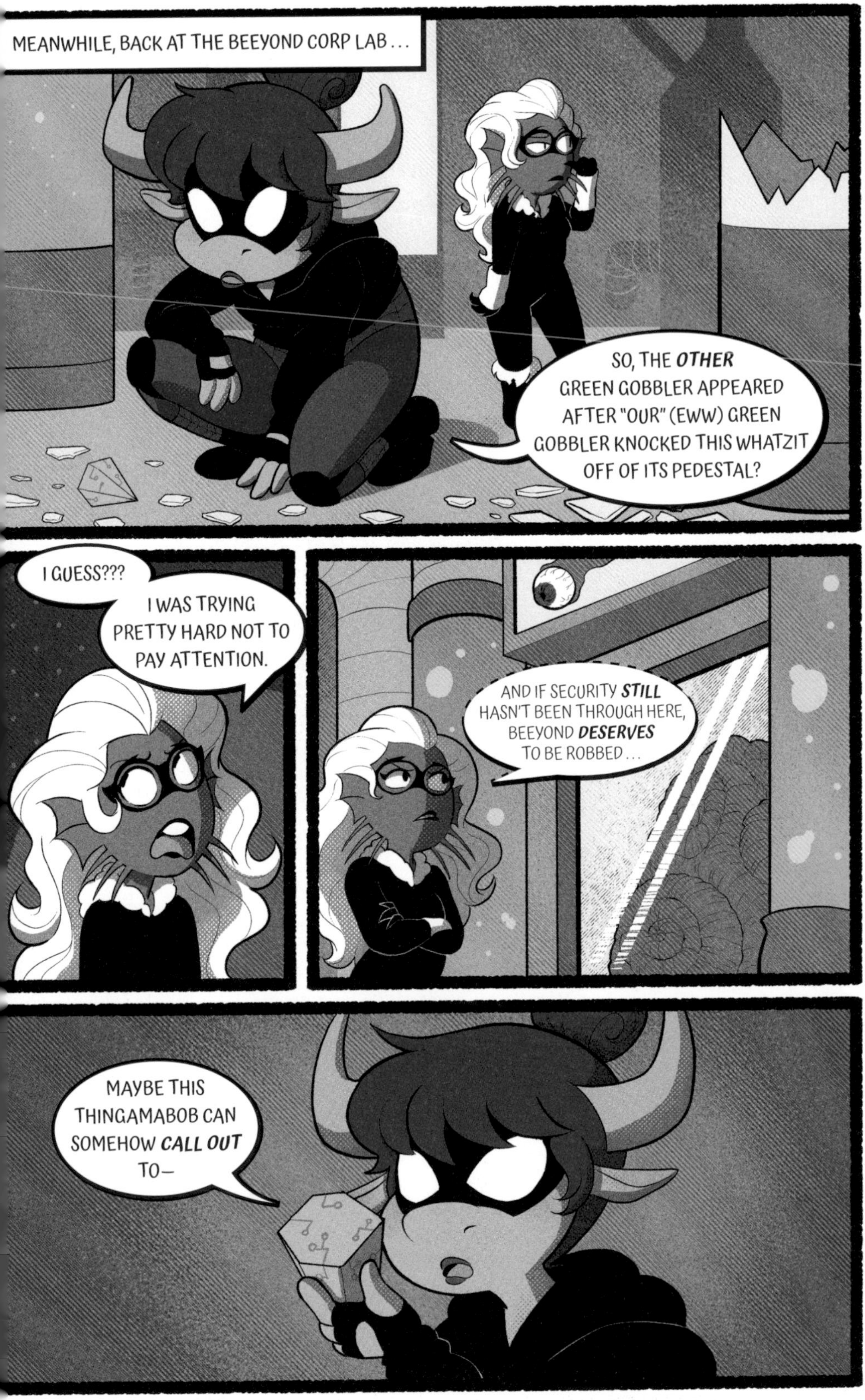

MEANWHILE, BACK AT THE BEEYOND CORP LAB . . .
SO, THE OTHER GREEN GOBBLER APPEARED AFTER "OUR" (EWW) GREEN GOBBLER KNOCKED THIS WHATZIT OFF OF ITS PEDESTAL?
I GUESS???
I WAS TRYING PRETTY HARD NOT TO PAY ATTENTION.
AND IF SECURITY STILL HASN'T BEEN THROUGH HERE, BEEYOND DESERVES TO BE ROBBED . . .
MAYBE THIS THINGAMABOB CAN SOMEHOW CALL OUT TO—

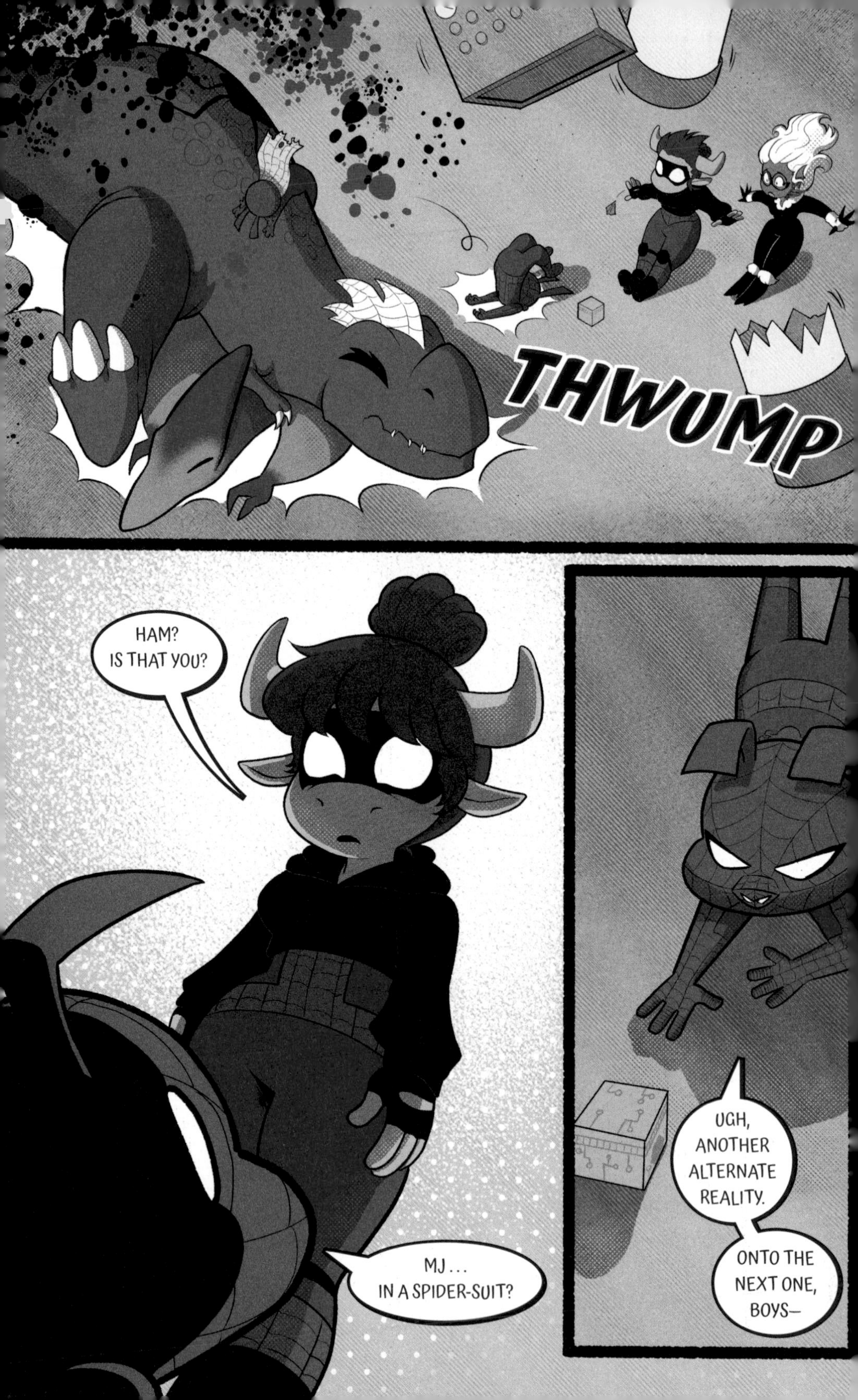
THWUMP
HAM? IS THAT YOU?
MJ . . . IN A SPIDER-SUIT?
UGH, ANOTHER ALTERNATE REALITY.
ONTO THE NEXT ONE, BOYS—

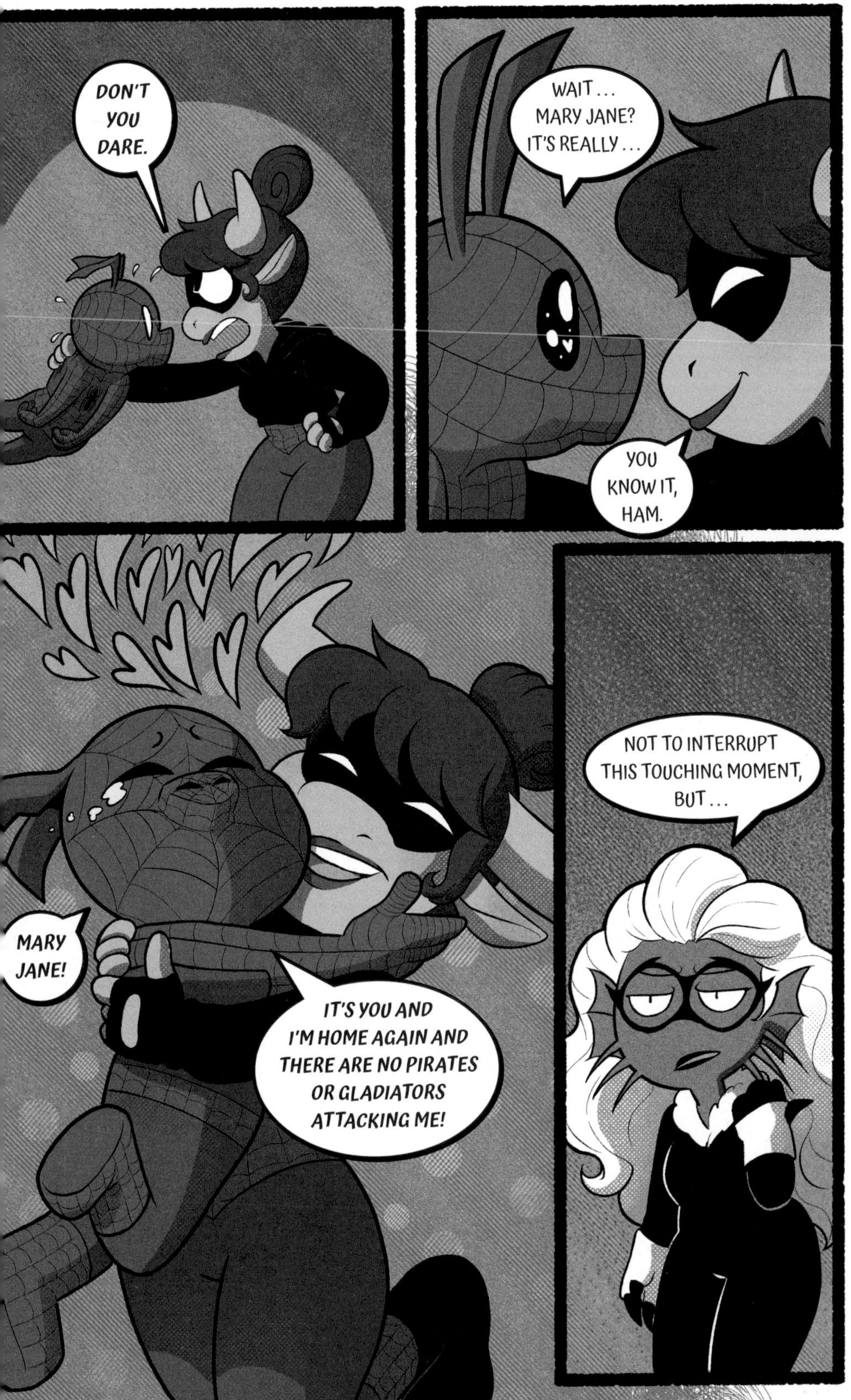
DON'T YOU DARE.
WAIT... MARY JANE? IT'S REALLY...
YOU KNOW IT, HAM.
NOT TO INTERRUPT THIS TOUCHING MOMENT, BUT...
MARY JANE!
IT'S YOU AND I'M HOME AGAIN AND THERE ARE NO PIRATES OR GLADIATORS ATTACKING ME!

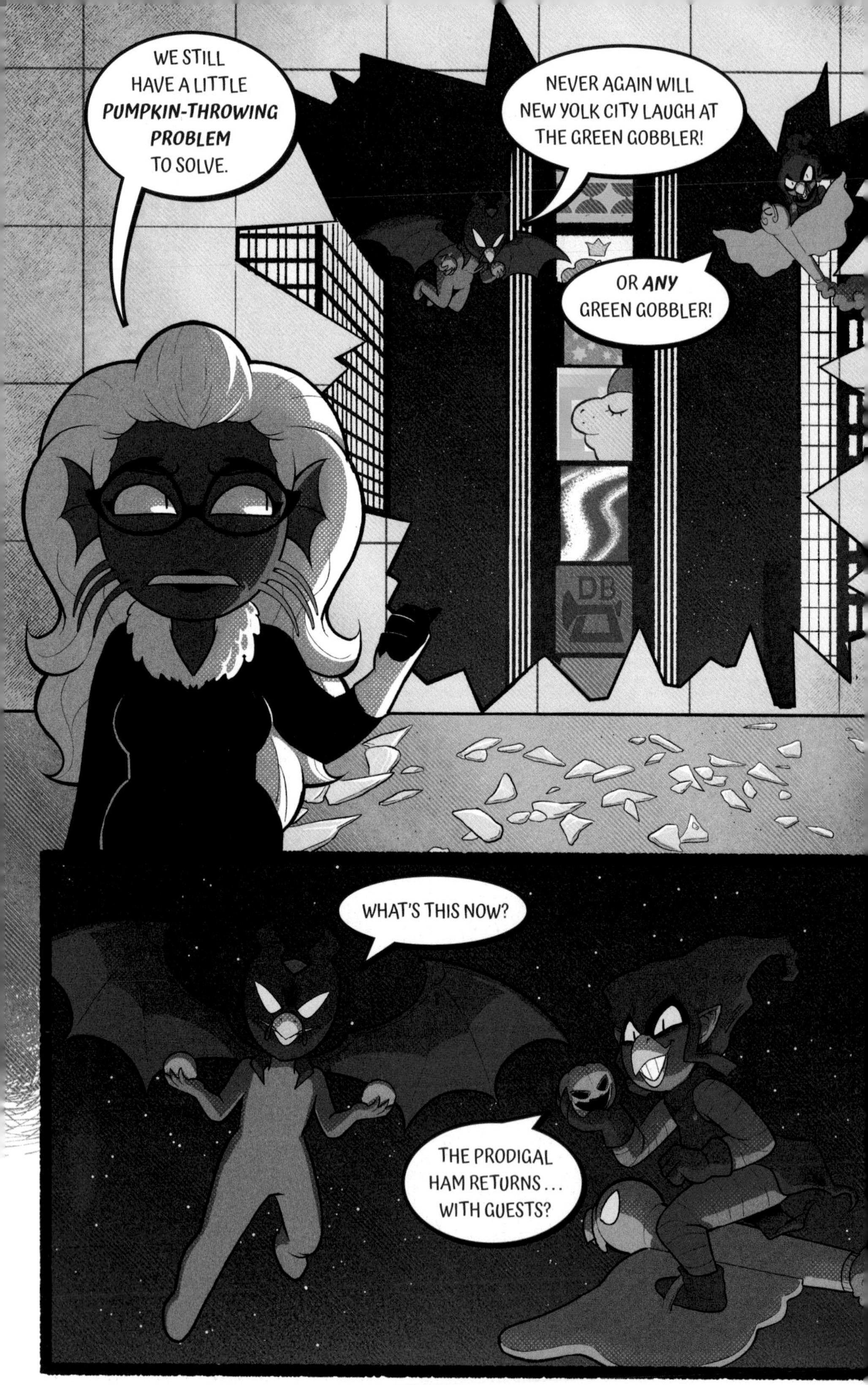
WE STILL HAVE A LITTLE **PUMPKIN-THROWING PROBLEM** TO SOLVE.
NEVER AGAIN WILL NEW YOLK CITY LAUGH AT THE GREEN GOBBLER!
OR *ANY* GREEN GOBBLER!
DB
WHAT'S THIS NOW?
THE PRODIGAL HAM RETURNS . . . WITH GUESTS?

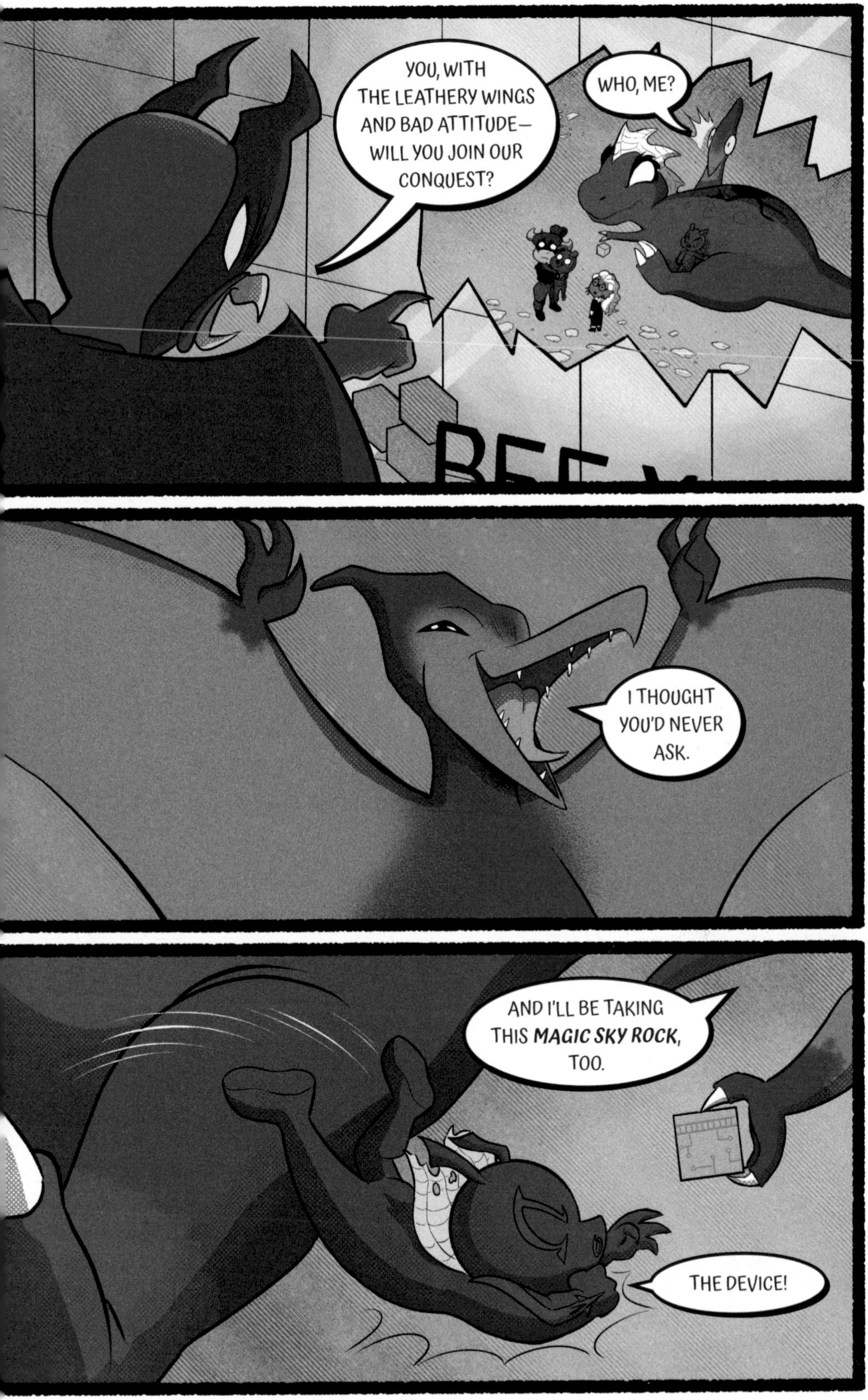
YOU, WITH THE LEATHERY WINGS AND BAD ATTITUDE—WILL YOU JOIN OUR CONQUEST?
WHO, ME?
I THOUGHT YOU'D NEVER ASK.
AND I'LL BE TAKING THIS ***MAGIC SKY ROCK***, TOO.
THE DEVICE!

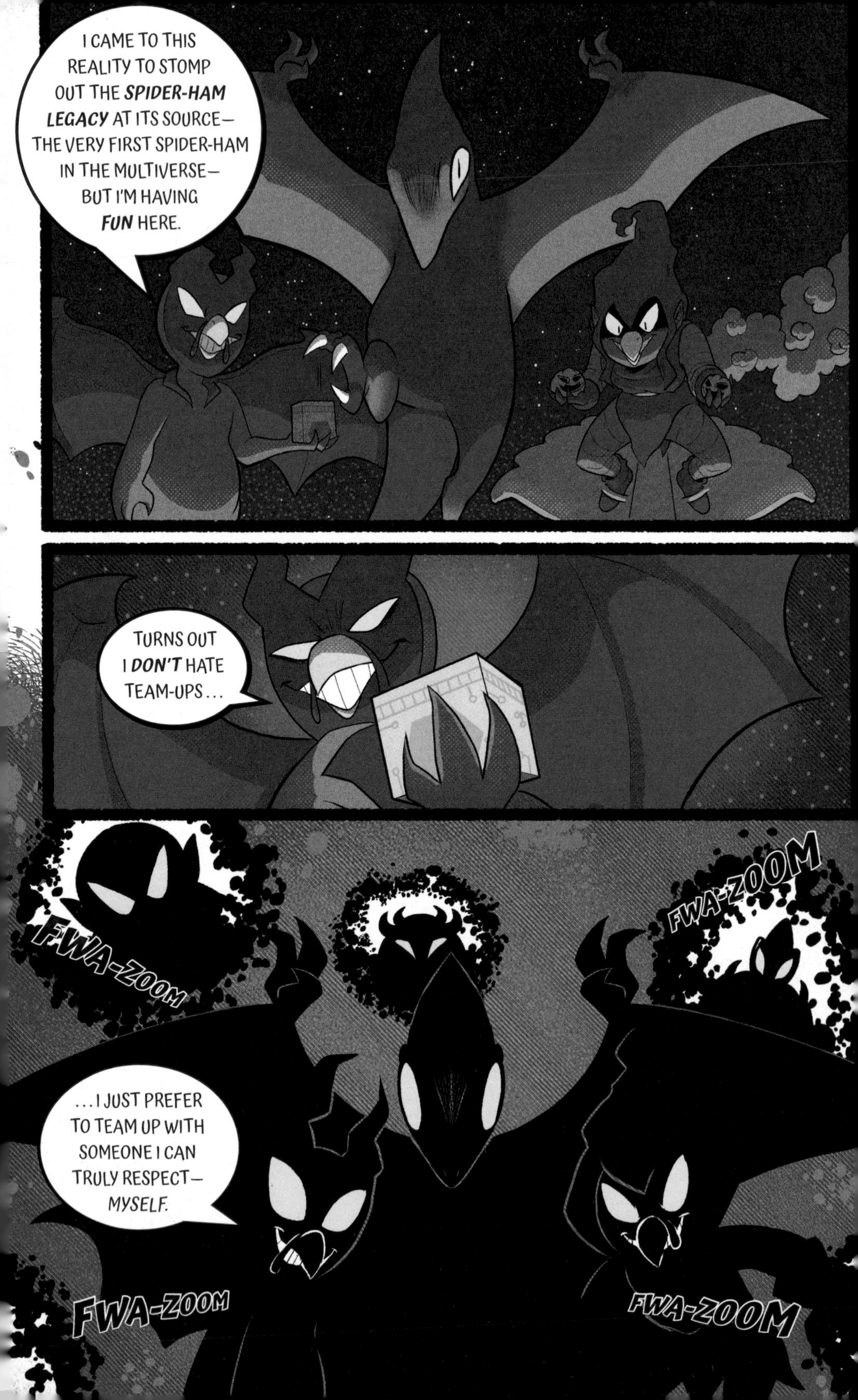
I CAME TO THIS REALITY TO STOMP OUT THE SPIDER-HAM LEGACY AT ITS SOURCE— THE VERY FIRST SPIDER-HAM IN THE MULTIVERSE— BUT I'M HAVING FUN HERE.
TURNS OUT I DON'T HATE TEAM-UPS...
FWA-ZOOM
FWA-ZOOM
...I JUST PREFER TO TEAM UP WITH SOMEONE I CAN TRULY RESPECT— MYSELF.
FWA-ZOOM
FWA-ZOOM

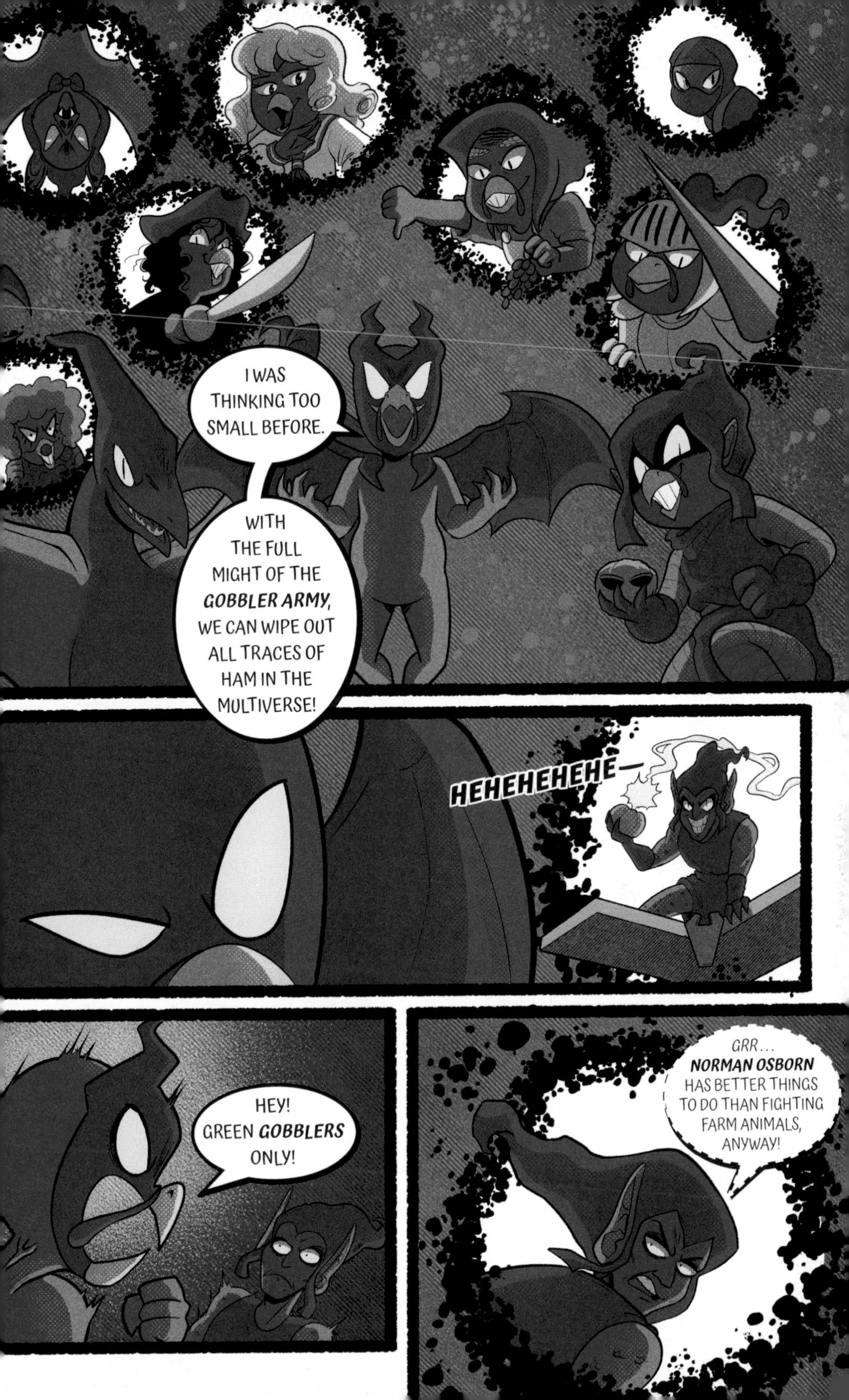
I WAS THINKING TOO SMALL BEFORE.
WITH THE FULL MIGHT OF THE ***GOBBLER ARMY***, WE CAN WIPE OUT ALL TRACES OF HAM IN THE MULTIVERSE!
HEHEHEHEHE—
HEY! GREEN ***GOBBLERS*** ONLY!
*GRR . . .* ***NORMAN OSBORN*** HAS BETTER THINGS TO DO THAN FIGHTING FARM ANIMALS, ANYWAY!

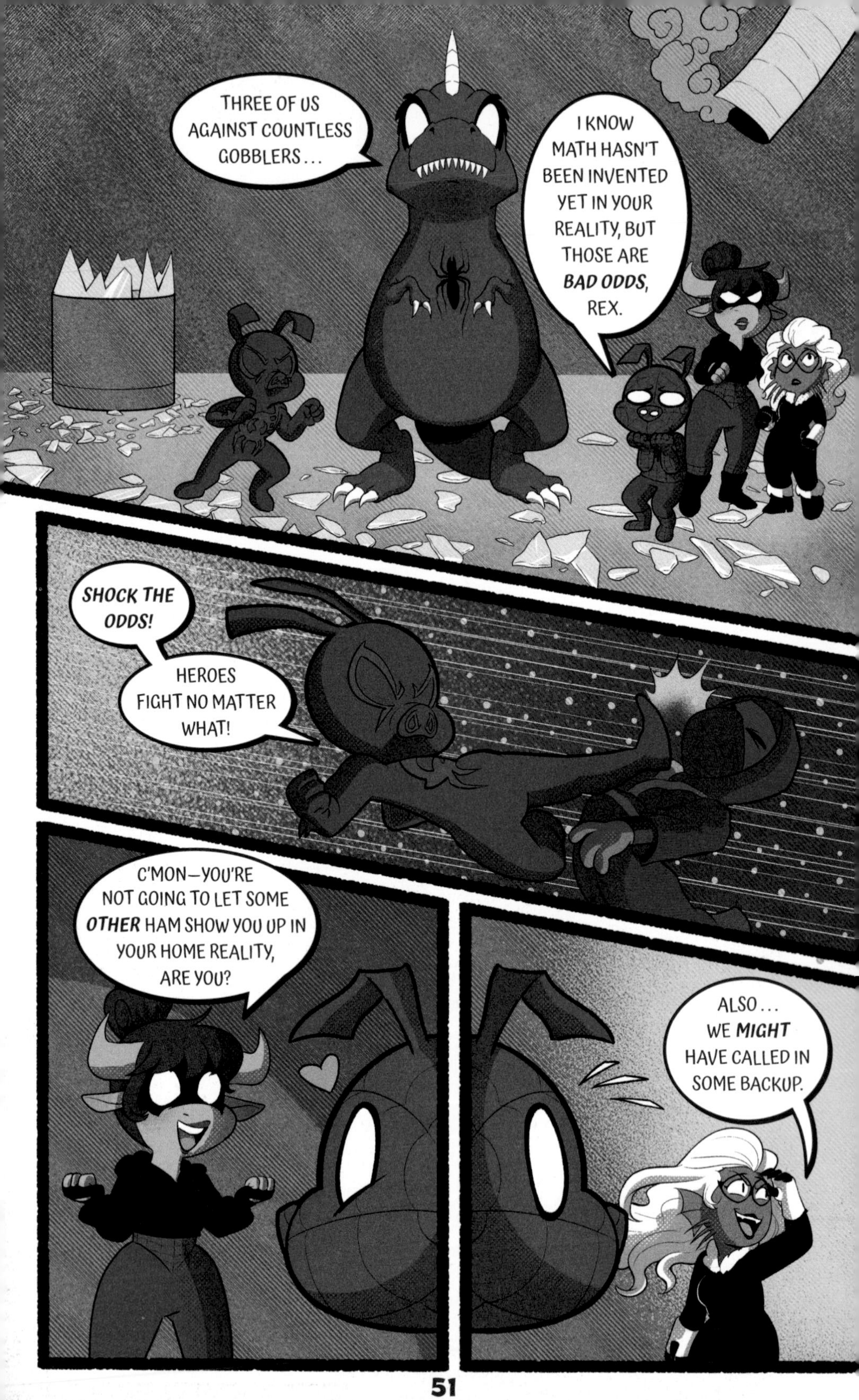
THREE OF US AGAINST COUNTLESS GOBBLERS . . .
I KNOW MATH HASN'T BEEN INVENTED YET IN YOUR REALITY, BUT THOSE ARE **BAD ODDS**, REX.
**SHOCK THE ODDS!**
HEROES FIGHT NO MATTER WHAT!
C'MON—YOU'RE NOT GOING TO LET SOME **OTHER** HAM SHOW YOU UP IN YOUR HOME REALITY, ARE YOU?
ALSO . . . WE **MIGHT** HAVE CALLED IN SOME BACKUP.

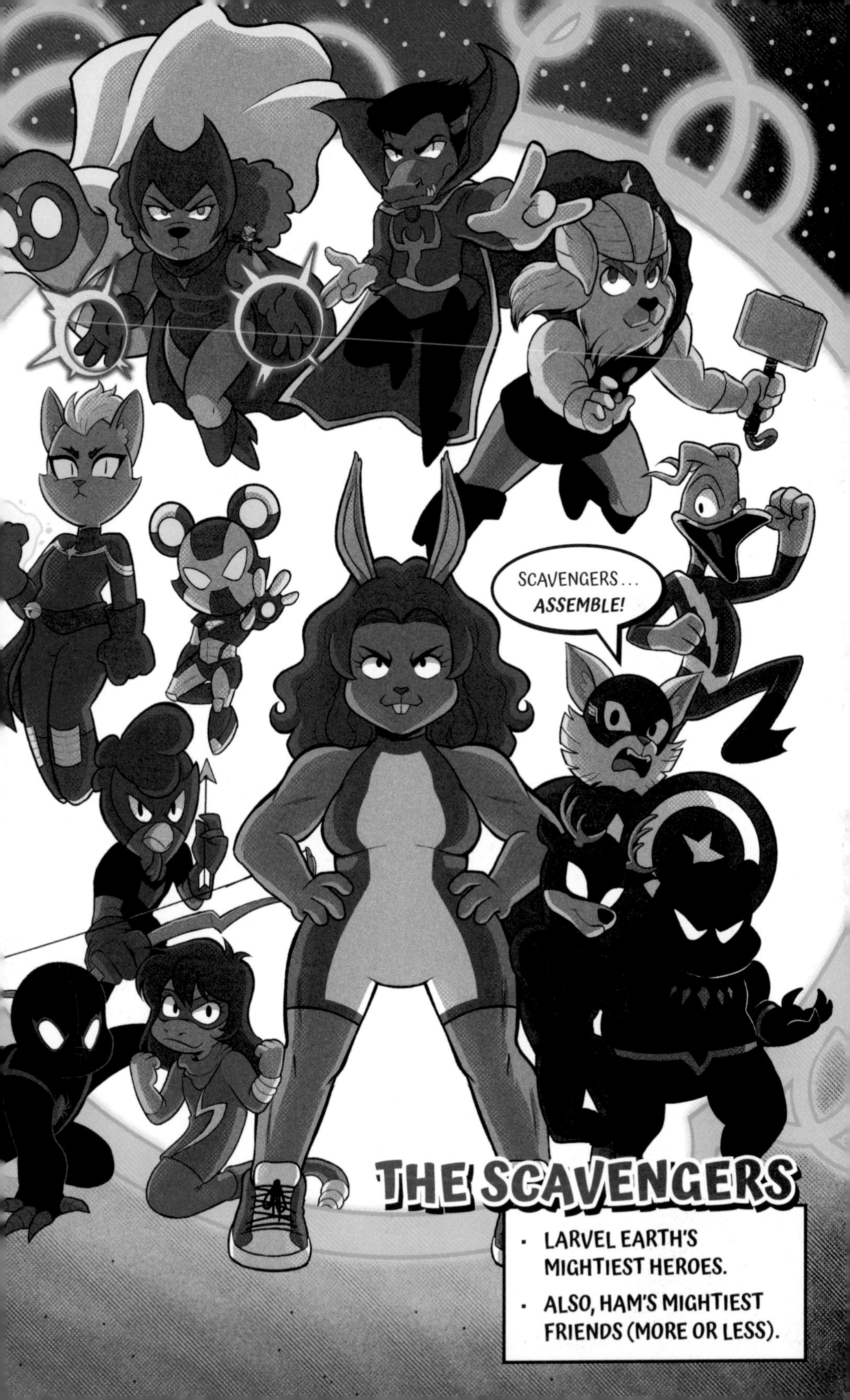

SCAVENGERS . . .
***ASSEMBLE!***
THE SCAVENGERS
- LARVEL EARTH'S MIGHTIEST HEROES.
- ALSO, HAM'S MIGHTIEST FRIENDS (MORE OR LESS).

# CHAPTER FIVE:
# FOWL PLAY!

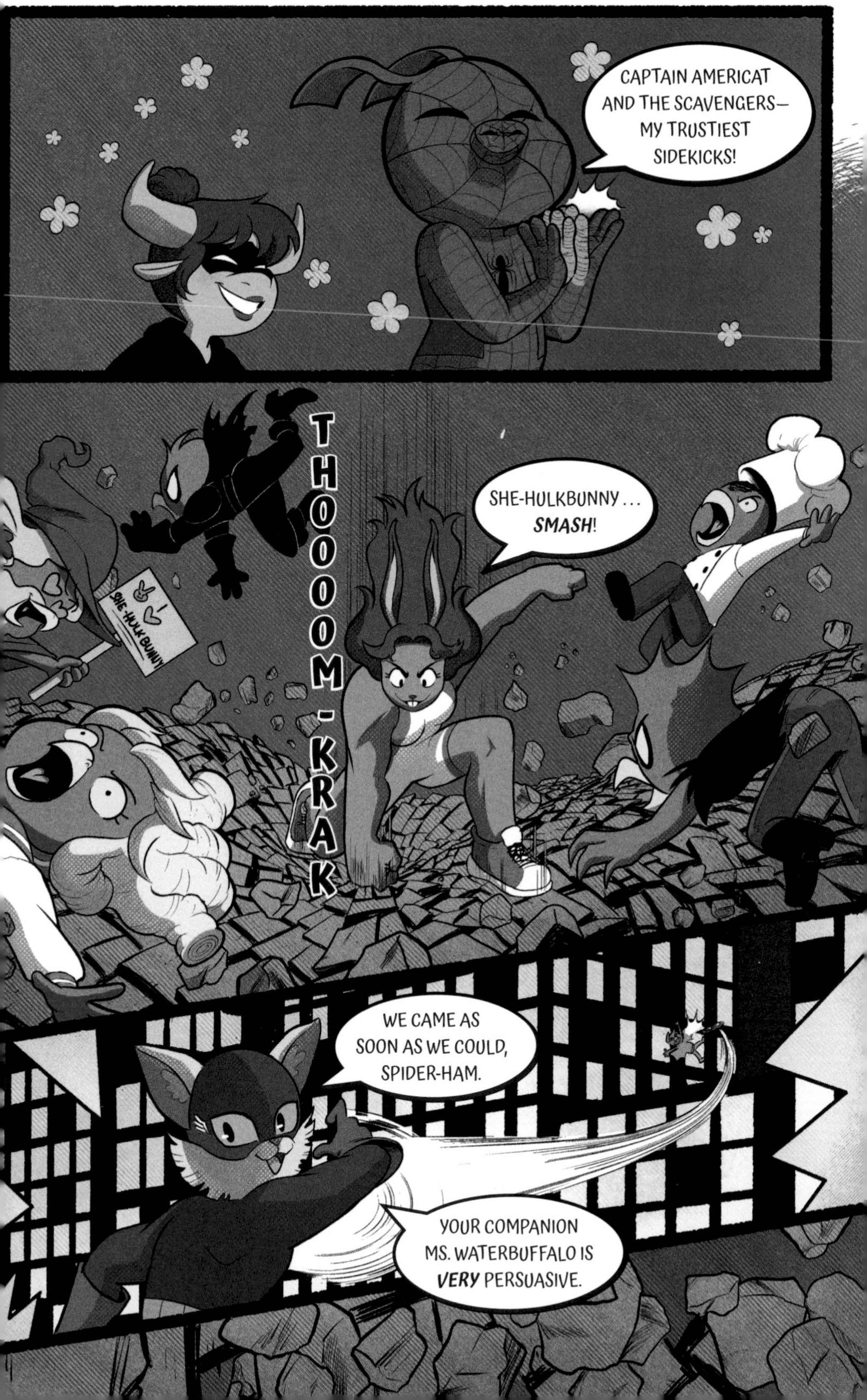
CAPTAIN AMERICAT AND THE SCAVENGERS—MY TRUSTIEST SIDEKICKS!
THOOOOOM-KRAK
SHE-HULKBUNNY . . . SMASH!
SHE-HULKBUNNY
WE CAME AS SOON AS WE COULD, SPIDER-HAM.
YOUR COMPANION MS. WATERBUFFALO IS VERY PERSUASIVE.

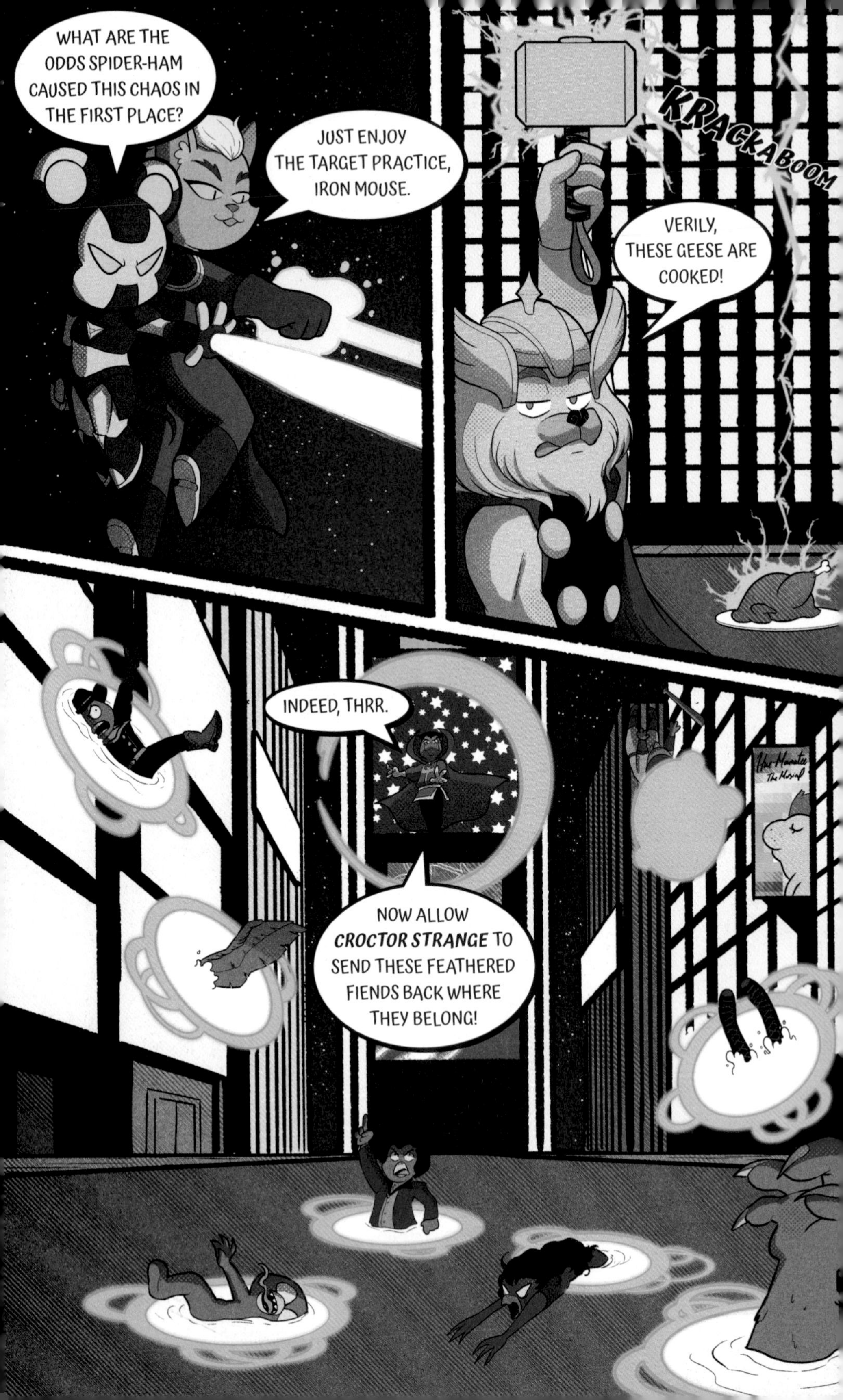
WHAT ARE THE ODDS SPIDER-HAM CAUSED THIS CHAOS IN THE FIRST PLACE?
JUST ENJOY THE TARGET PRACTICE, IRON MOUSE.
KRACKABOOM
VERILY, THESE GEESE ARE COOKED!
INDEED, THRR.
NOW ALLOW *CROCTOR STRANGE* TO SEND THESE FEATHERED FIENDS BACK WHERE THEY BELONG!

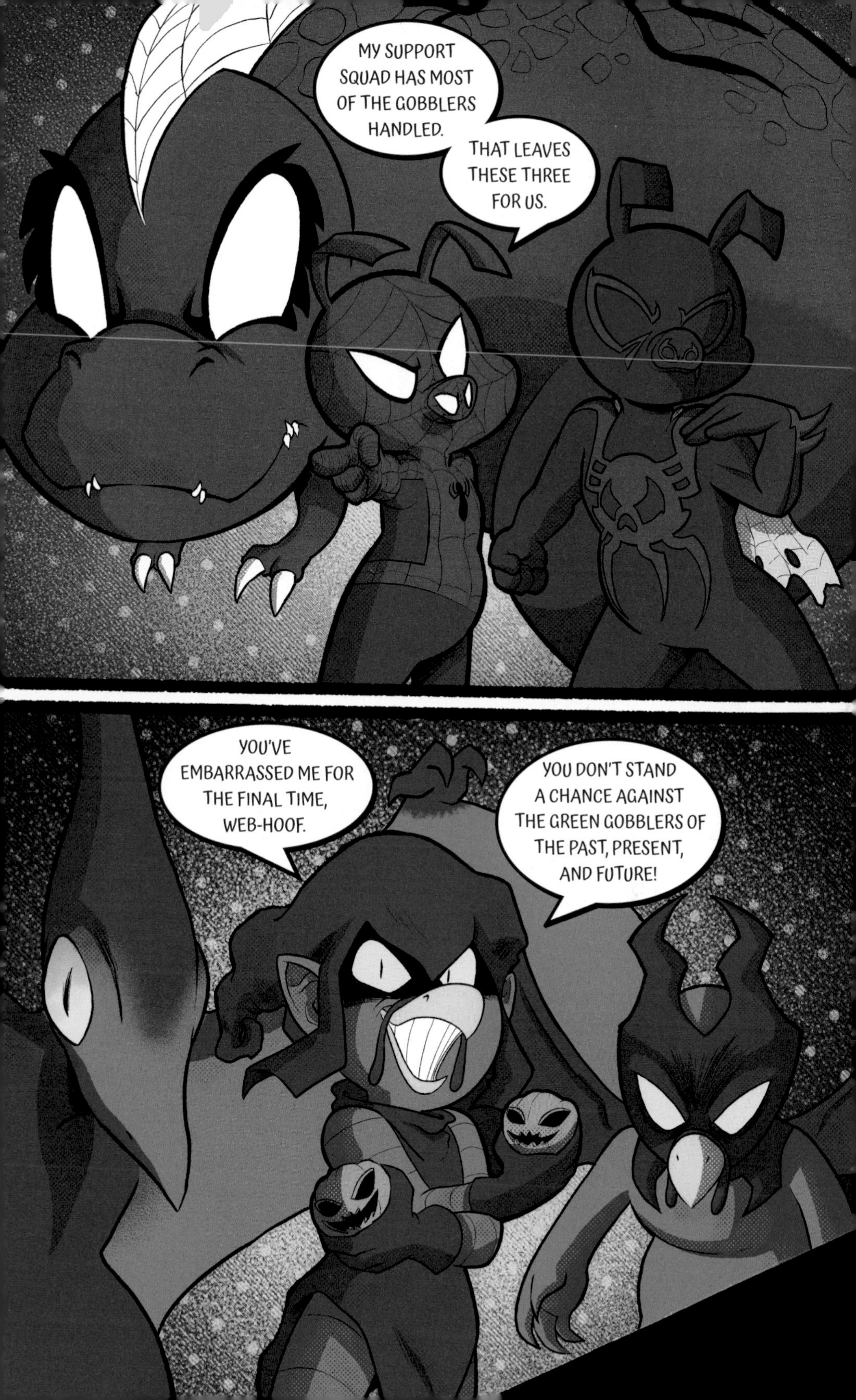
MY SUPPORT SQUAD HAS MOST OF THE GOBBLERS HANDLED.
THAT LEAVES THESE THREE FOR US.
YOU'VE EMBARRASSED ME FOR THE FINAL TIME, WEB-HOOF.
YOU DON'T STAND A CHANCE AGAINST THE GREEN GOBBLERS OF THE PAST, PRESENT, AND FUTURE!

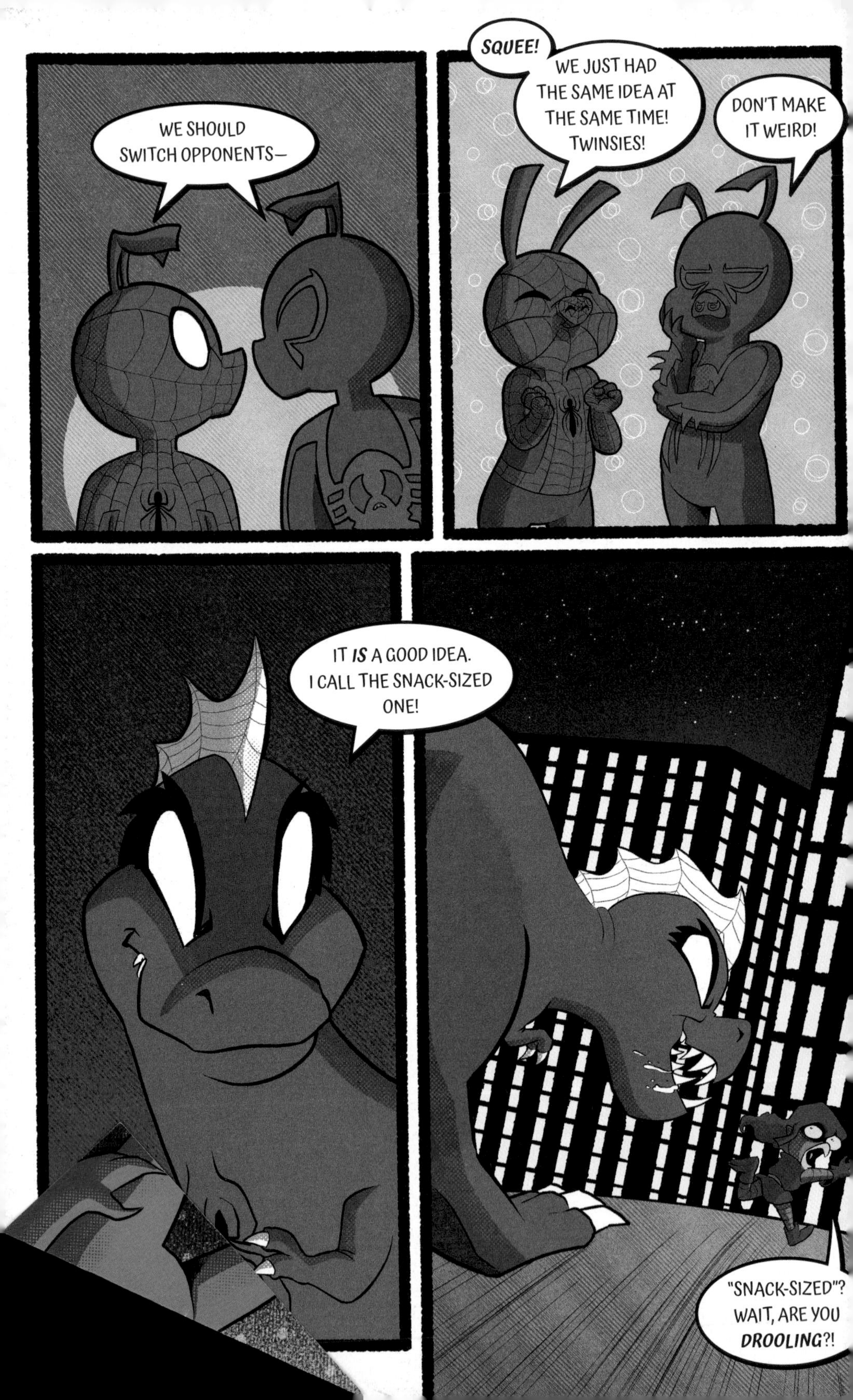
WE SHOULD SWITCH OPPONENTS—
SQUEE!
WE JUST HAD THE SAME IDEA AT THE SAME TIME! TWINSIES!
DON'T MAKE IT WEIRD!
IT *IS* A GOOD IDEA. I CALL THE SNACK-SIZED ONE!
"SNACK-SIZED"? WAIT, ARE YOU *DROOLING*?!

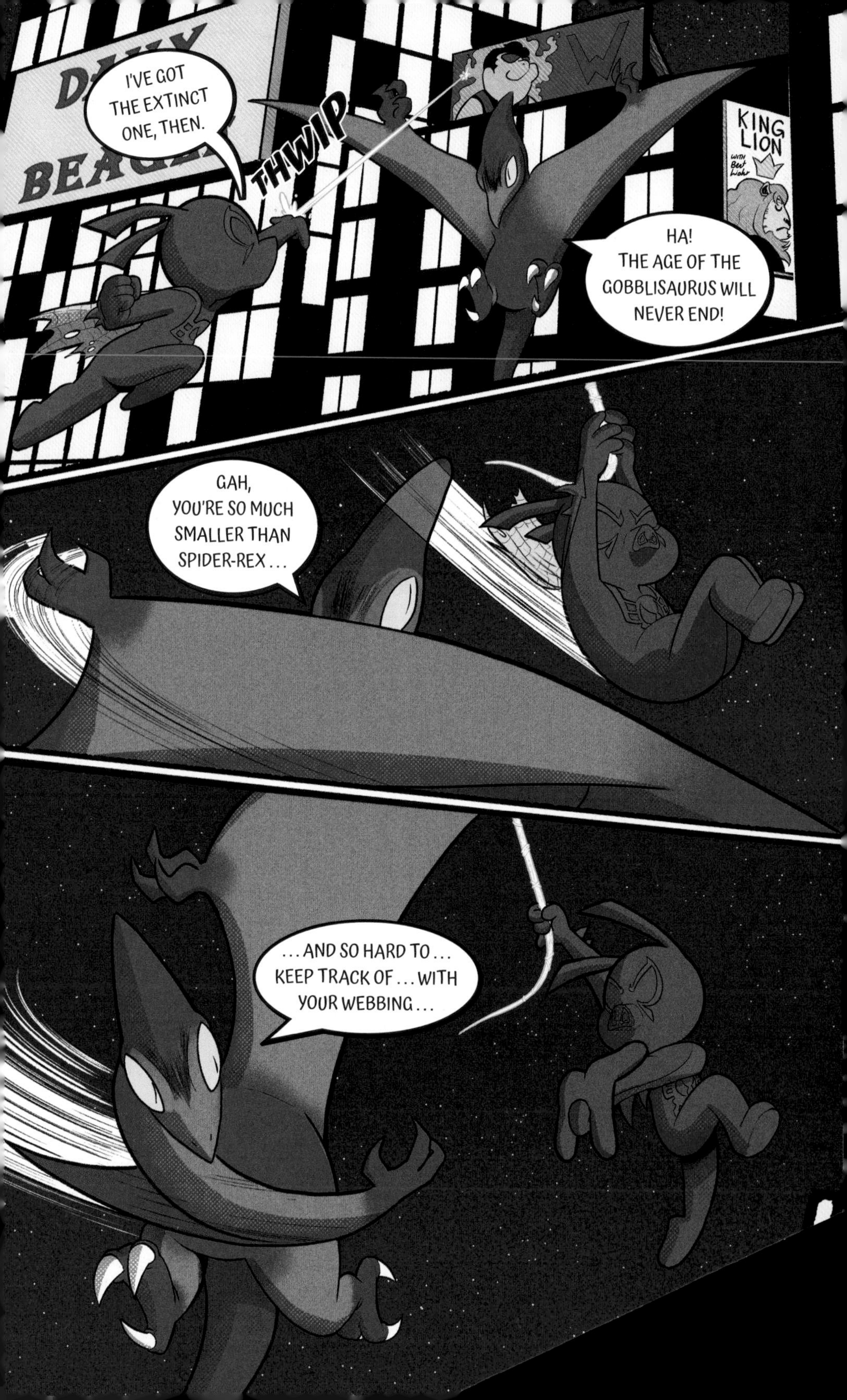
DAILY BEAGLE
KING LION WITH Bert Lahr
I'VE GOT THE EXTINCT ONE, THEN.
THWIP
HA! THE AGE OF THE GOBBLISAURUS WILL NEVER END!
GAH, YOU'RE SO MUCH SMALLER THAN SPIDER-REX . . .
. . . AND SO HARD TO . . . KEEP TRACK OF . . . WITH YOUR WEBBING . . .

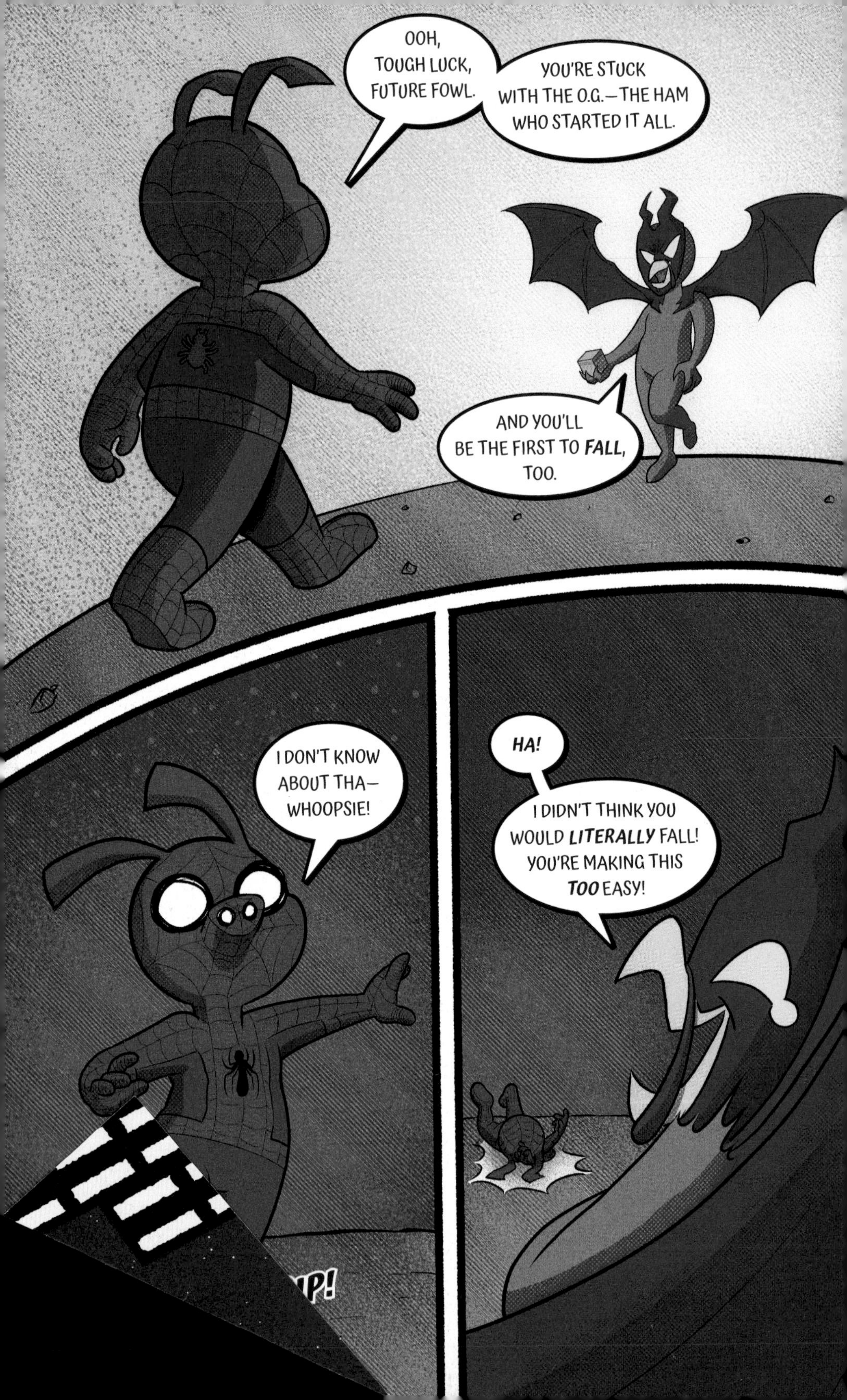
OOH, TOUGH LUCK, FUTURE FOWL.
YOU'RE STUCK WITH THE O.G.—THE HAM WHO STARTED IT ALL.
AND YOU'LL BE THE FIRST TO FALL, TOO.
I DON'T KNOW ABOUT THA— WHOOPSIE!
HA!
I DIDN'T THINK YOU WOULD LITERALLY FALL! YOU'RE MAKING THIS TOO EASY!

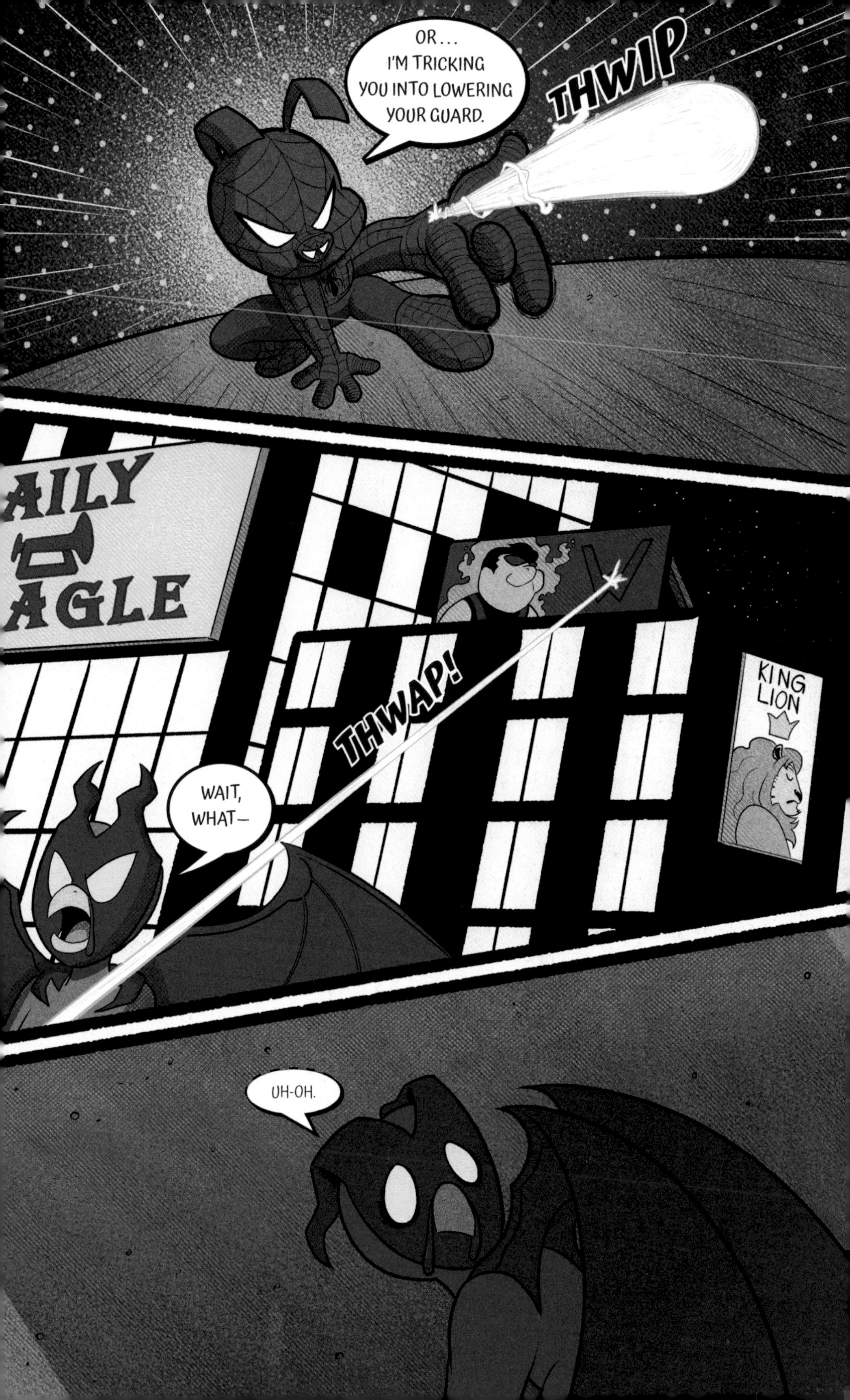
OR . . .
I'M TRICKING
YOU INTO LOWERING
YOUR GUARD.
THWIP
AILY
AGLE
KING
LION
THWAP!
WAIT,
WHAT—
UH-OH.

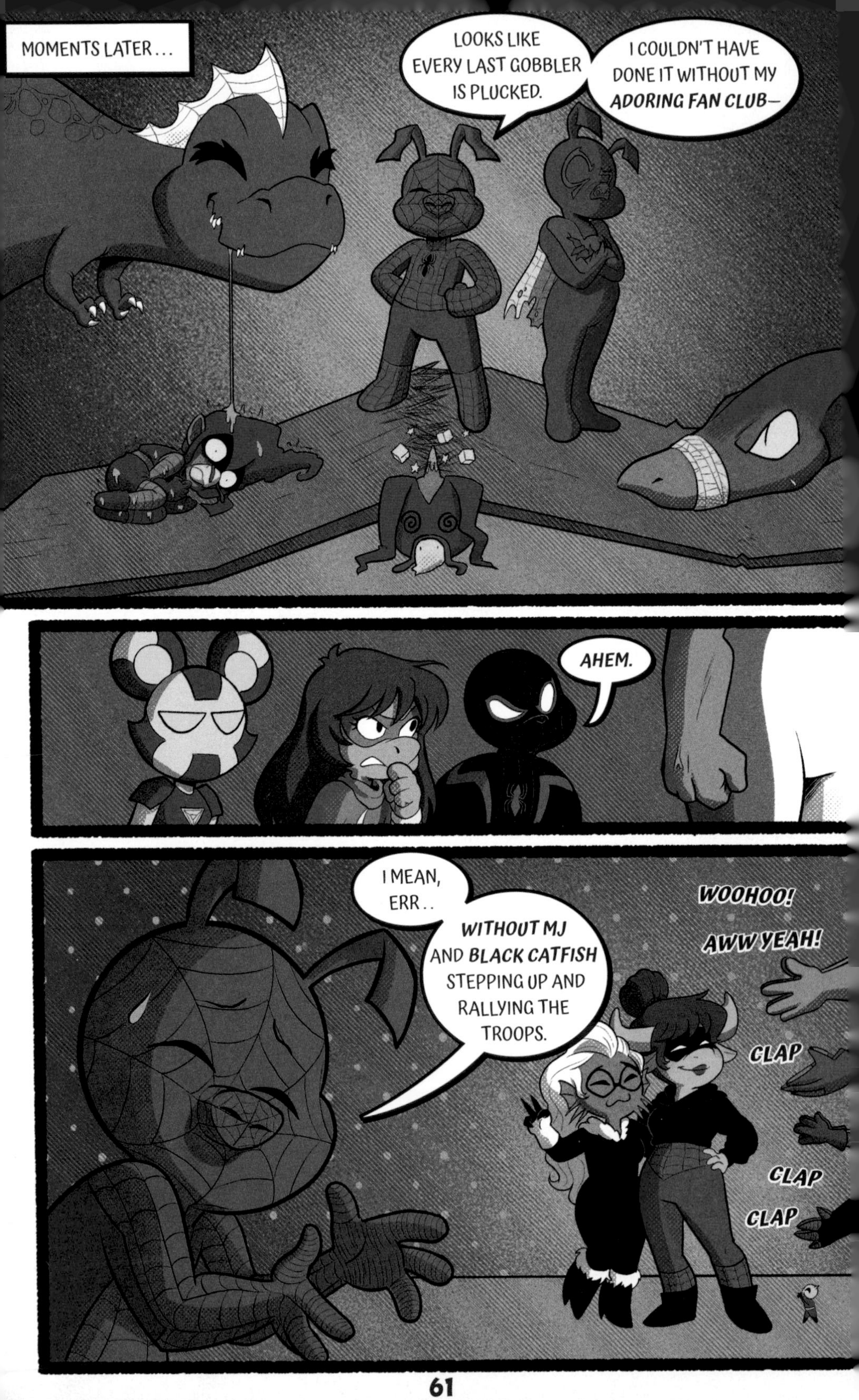
MOMENTS LATER...
LOOKS LIKE EVERY LAST GOBBLER IS PLUCKED.
I COULDN'T HAVE DONE IT WITHOUT MY ADORING FAN CLUB—
AHEM.
I MEAN, ERR..
WITHOUT MJ AND BLACK CATFISH STEPPING UP AND RALLYING THE TROOPS.
WOOHOO!
AWW YEAH!
CLAP
CLAP
CLAP

# EPILOGUE:
# HOG-FELT GOODBYES!

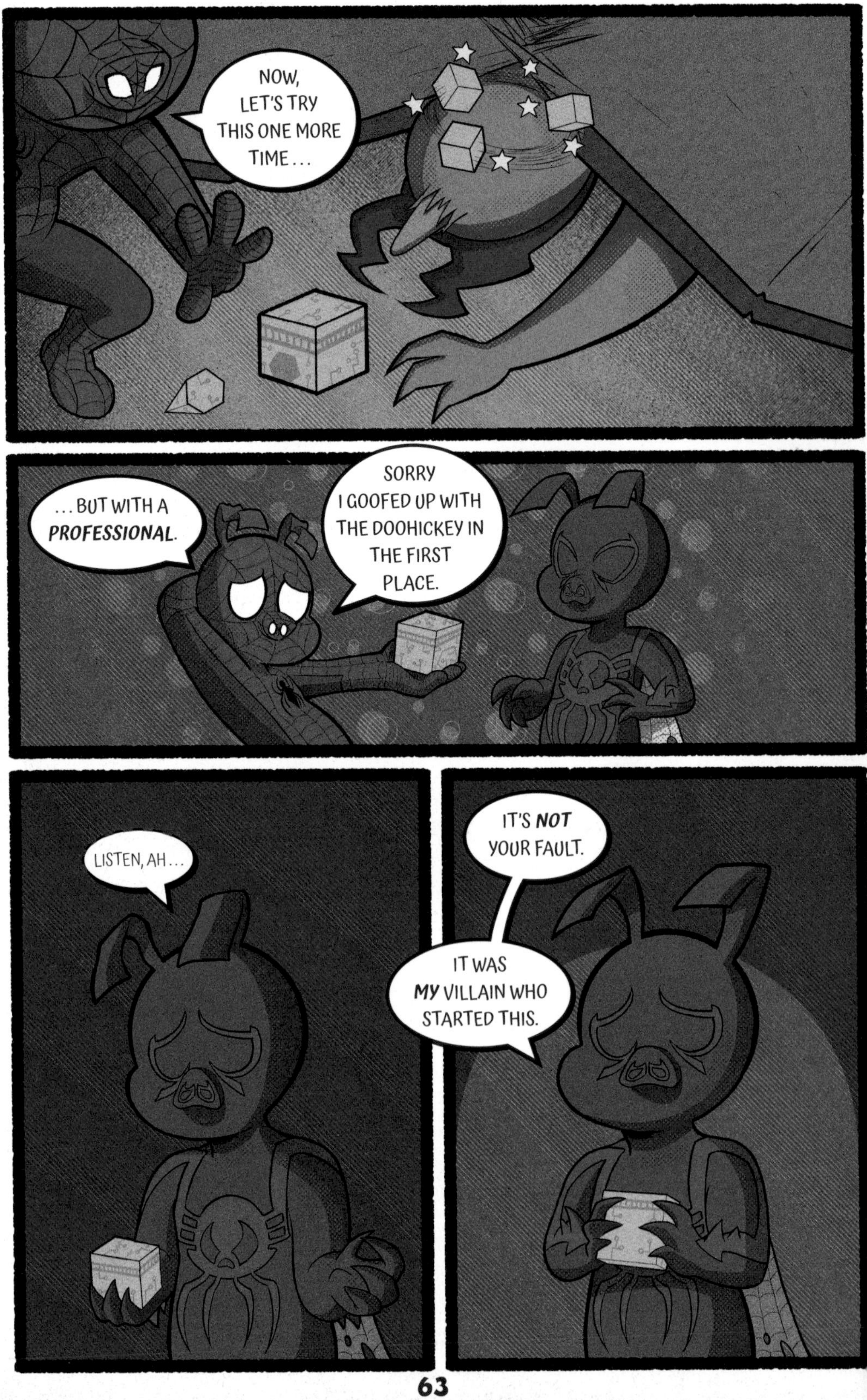
NOW, LET'S TRY THIS ONE MORE TIME . . .
. . . BUT WITH A **PROFESSIONAL**.
SORRY I GOOFED UP WITH THE DOOHICKEY IN THE FIRST PLACE.
LISTEN, AH . . .
IT'S **NOT** YOUR FAULT.
IT WAS **MY** VILLAIN WHO STARTED THIS.

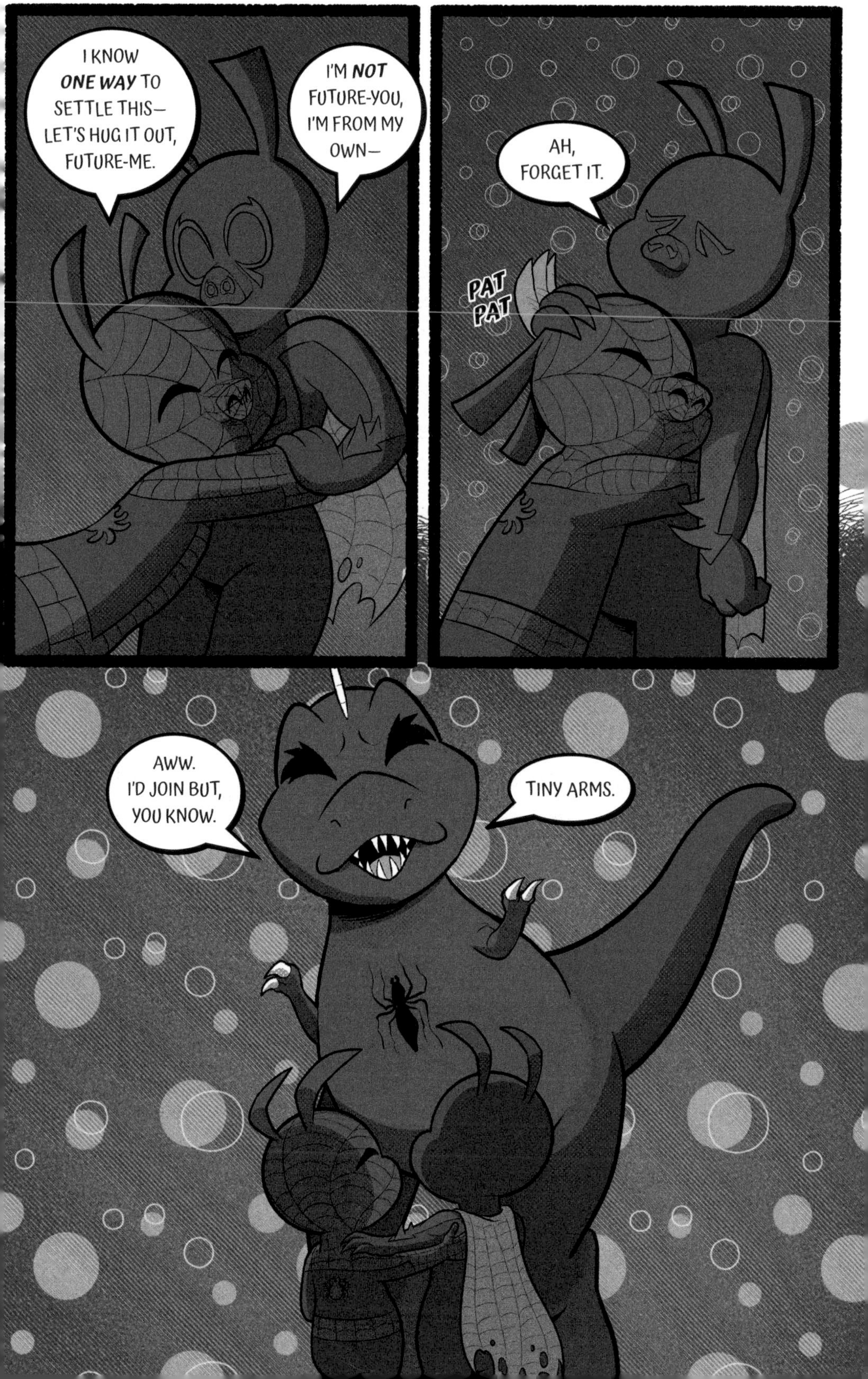
I KNOW ONE WAY TO SETTLE THIS— LET'S HUG IT OUT, FUTURE-ME.
I'M NOT FUTURE-YOU, I'M FROM MY OWN—
AH, FORGET IT.
PAT PAT
AWW. I'D JOIN BUT, YOU KNOW.
TINY ARMS.

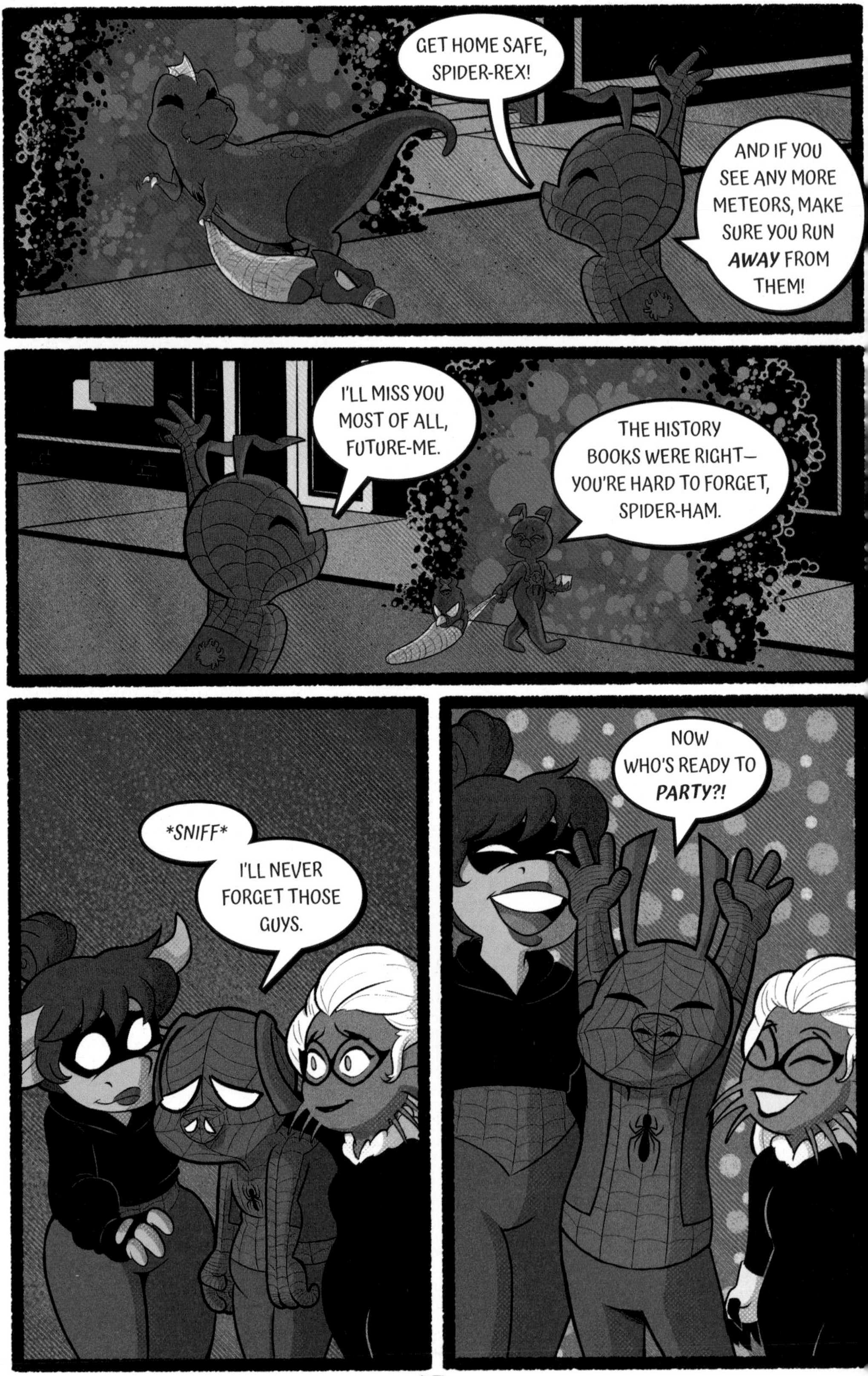
GET HOME SAFE, SPIDER-REX!
AND IF YOU SEE ANY MORE METEORS, MAKE SURE YOU RUN **AWAY** FROM THEM!
I'LL MISS YOU MOST OF ALL, FUTURE-ME.
THE HISTORY BOOKS WERE RIGHT— YOU'RE HARD TO FORGET, SPIDER-HAM.
*SNIFF*
I'LL NEVER FORGET THOSE GUYS.
NOW WHO'S READY TO **PARTY?!**

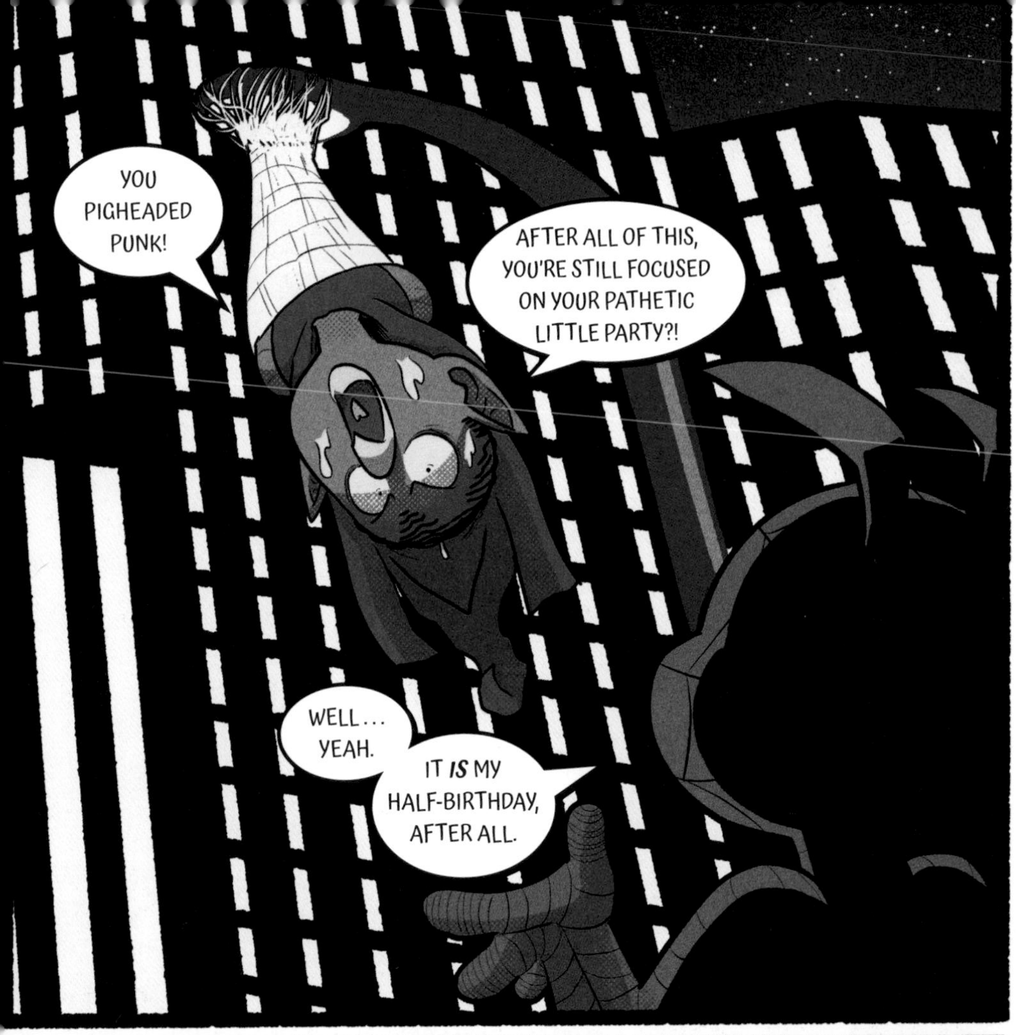
YOU PIGHEADED PUNK!
AFTER ALL OF THIS, YOU'RE STILL FOCUSED ON YOUR PATHETIC LITTLE PARTY?!
WELL . . . YEAH.
IT *IS* MY HALF-BIRTHDAY, AFTER ALL.

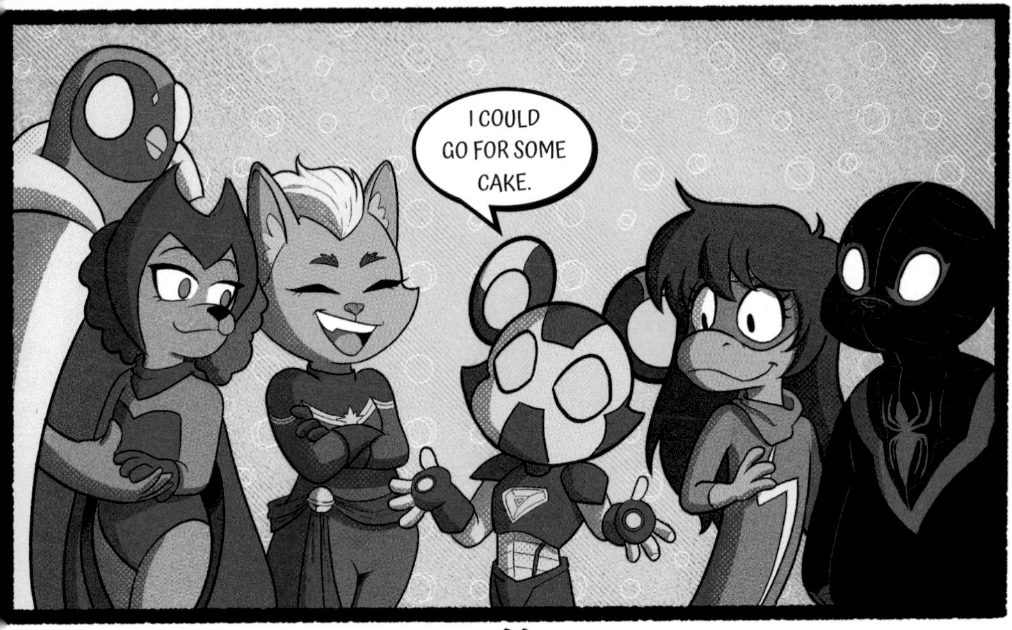
I COULD GO FOR SOME CAKE.

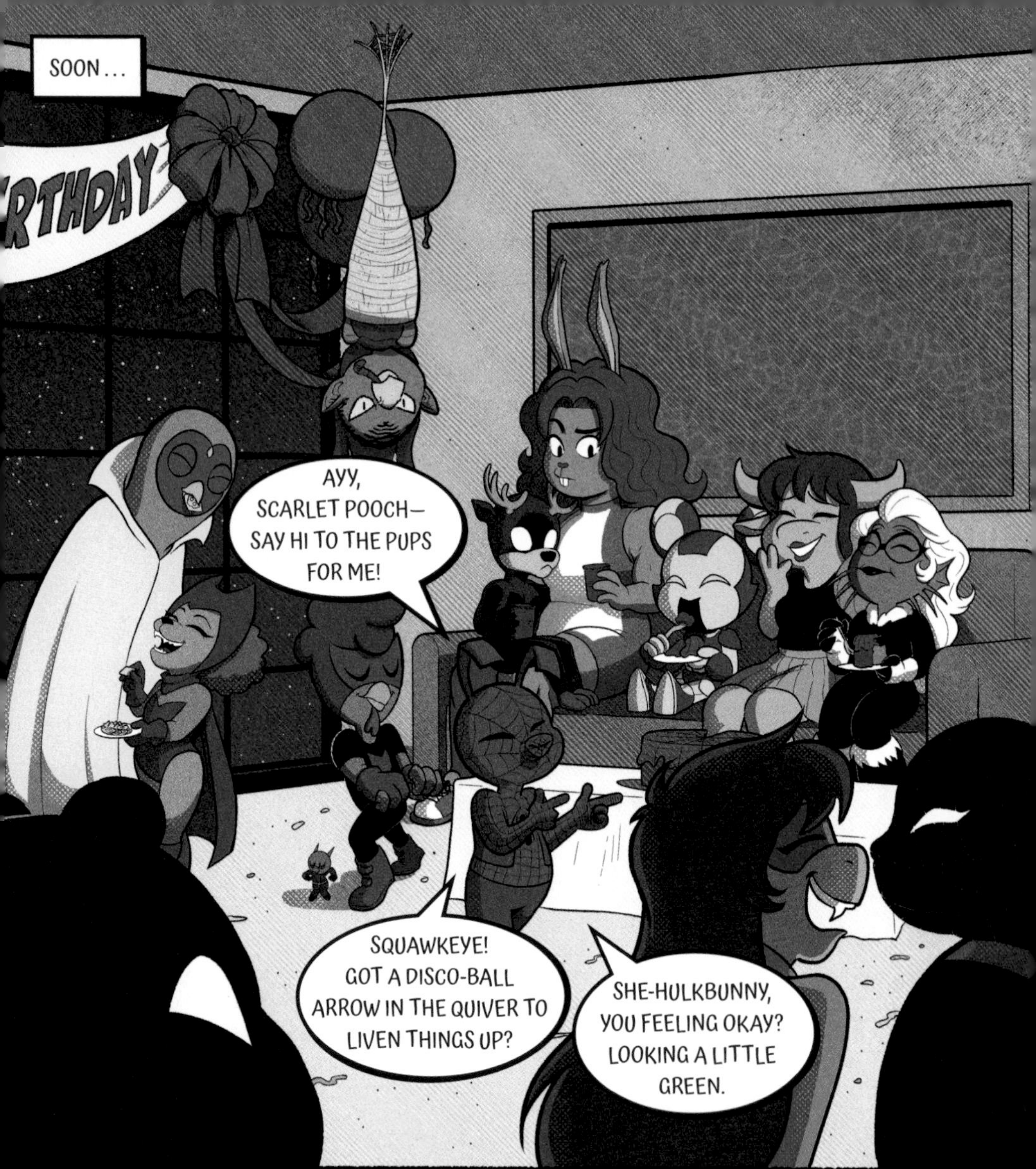
SOON...
RTHDAY
AYY, SCARLET POOCH— SAY HI TO THE PUPS FOR ME!
SQUAWKEYE! GOT A DISCO-BALL ARROW IN THE QUIVER TO LIVEN THINGS UP?
SHE-HULKBUNNY, YOU FEELING OKAY? LOOKING A LITTLE GREEN.

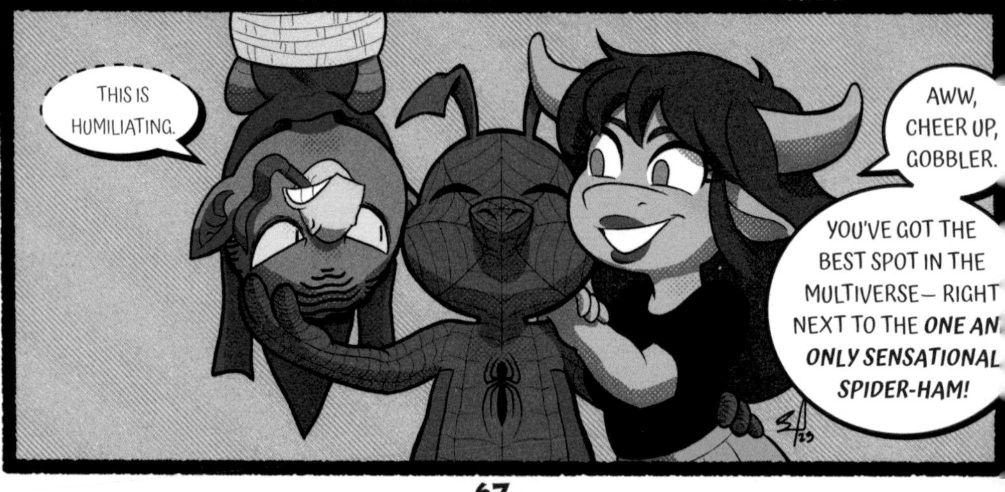
THIS IS HUMILIATING.
AWW, CHEER UP, GOBBLER.
YOU'VE GOT THE BEST SPOT IN THE MULTIVERSE— RIGHT NEXT TO THE ***ONE AN ONLY SENSATIONAL SPIDER-HAM!***

# THE END!

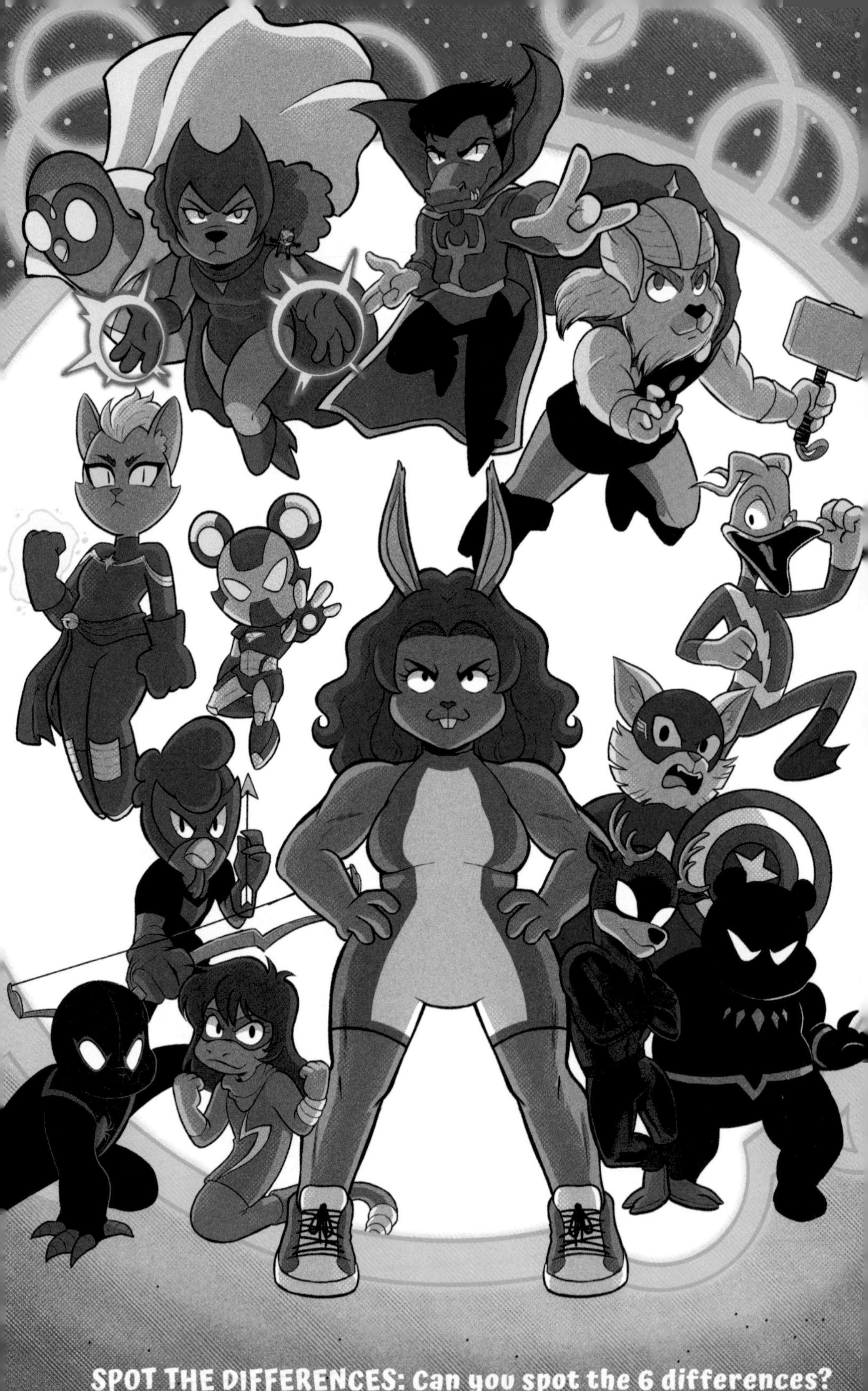

**SPOT THE DIFFERENCES: Can you spot the 6 differences?**

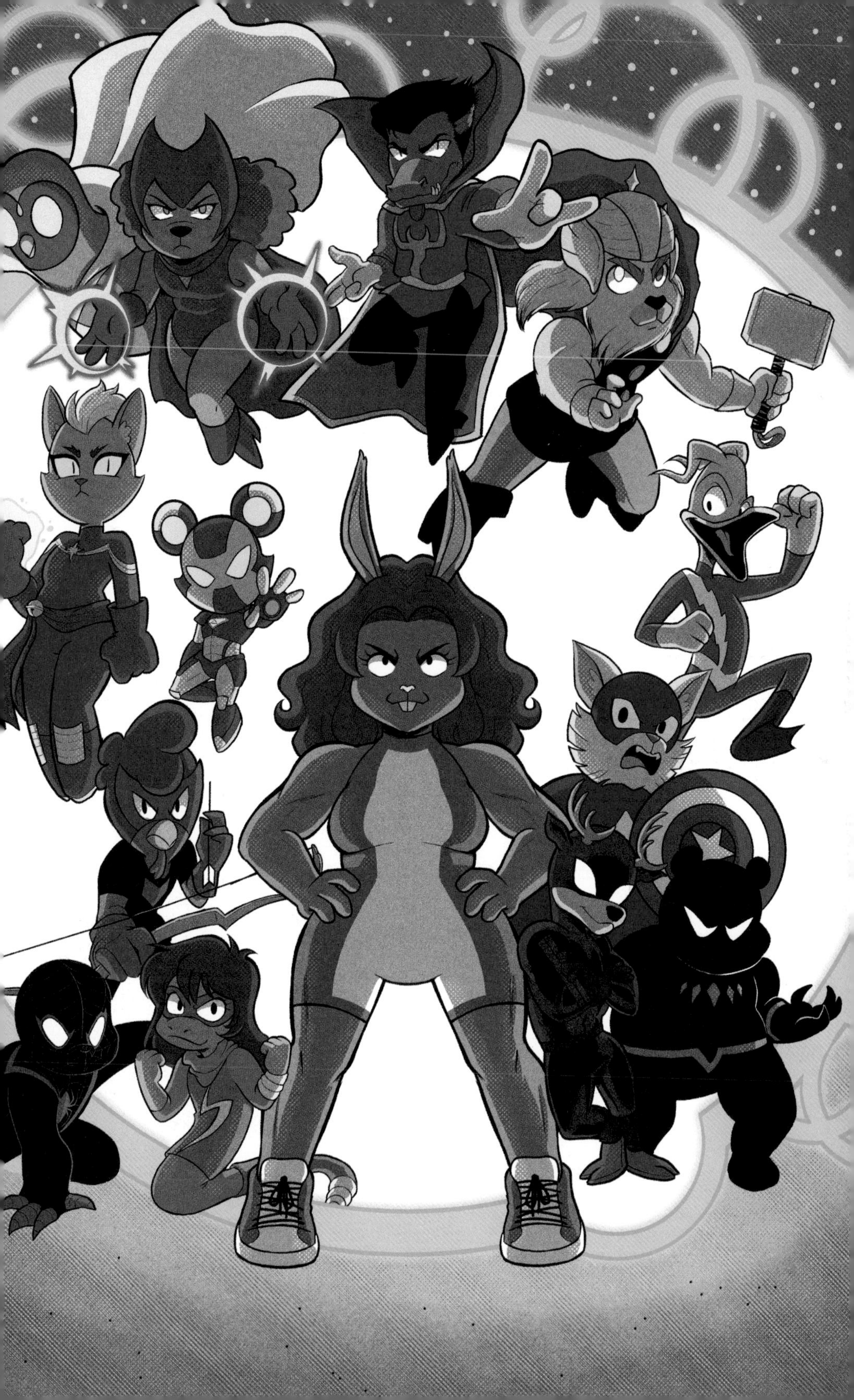

# SPECIAL PREVIEW OF:

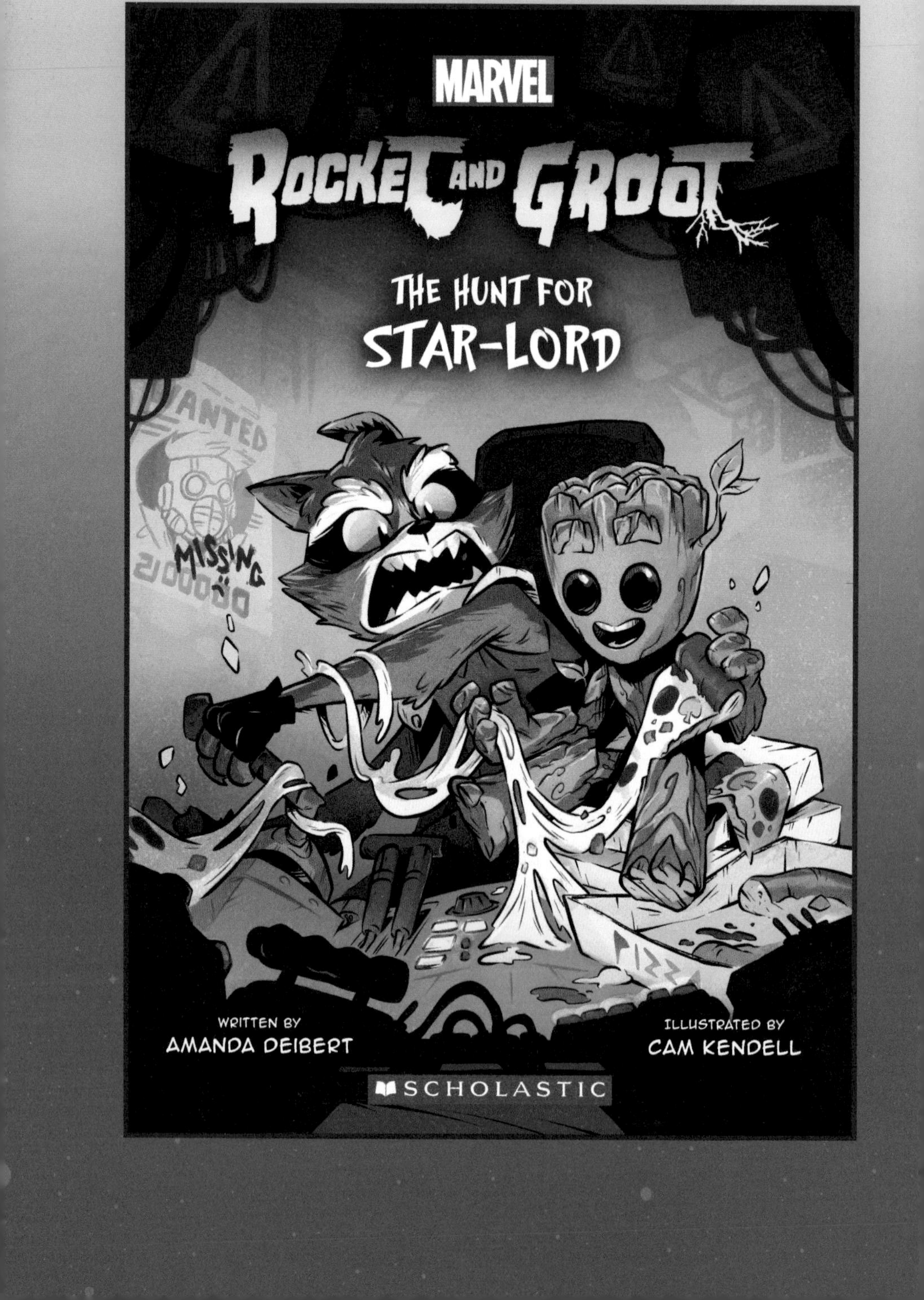
MARVEL
ROCKET AND GROOT
THE HUNT FOR
STAR-LORD
MISSING
WRITTEN BY
AMANDA DEIBERT
ILLUSTRATED BY
CAM KENDELL
SCHOLASTIC

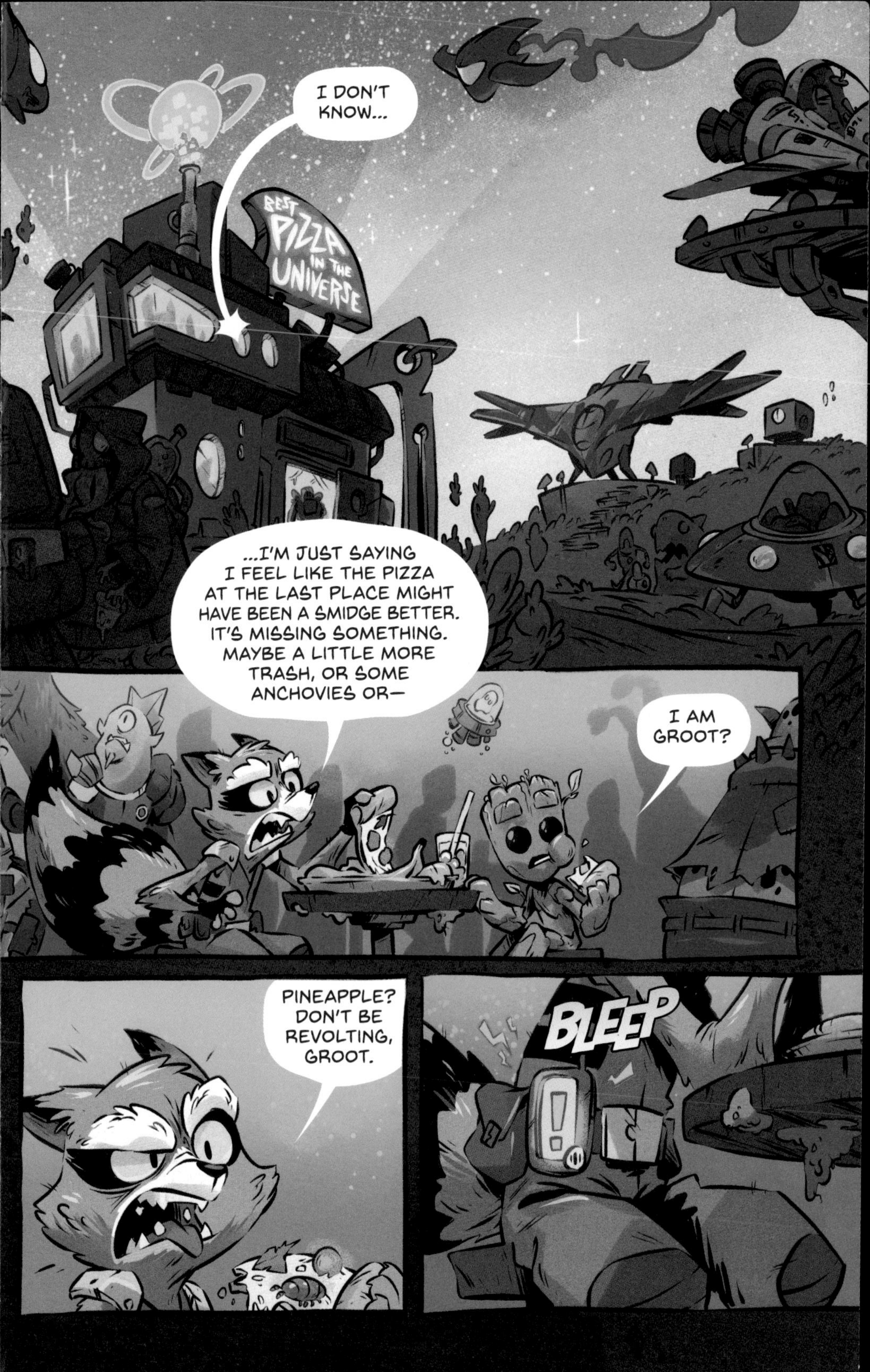
I DON'T KNOW...
BEST PIZZA IN THE UNIVERSE
...I'M JUST SAYING I FEEL LIKE THE PIZZA AT THE LAST PLACE MIGHT HAVE BEEN A SMIDGE BETTER. IT'S MISSING SOMETHING. MAYBE A LITTLE MORE TRASH, OR SOME ANCHOVIES OR—
I AM GROOT?
PINEAPPLE? DON'T BE REVOLTING, GROOT.
BLEEP

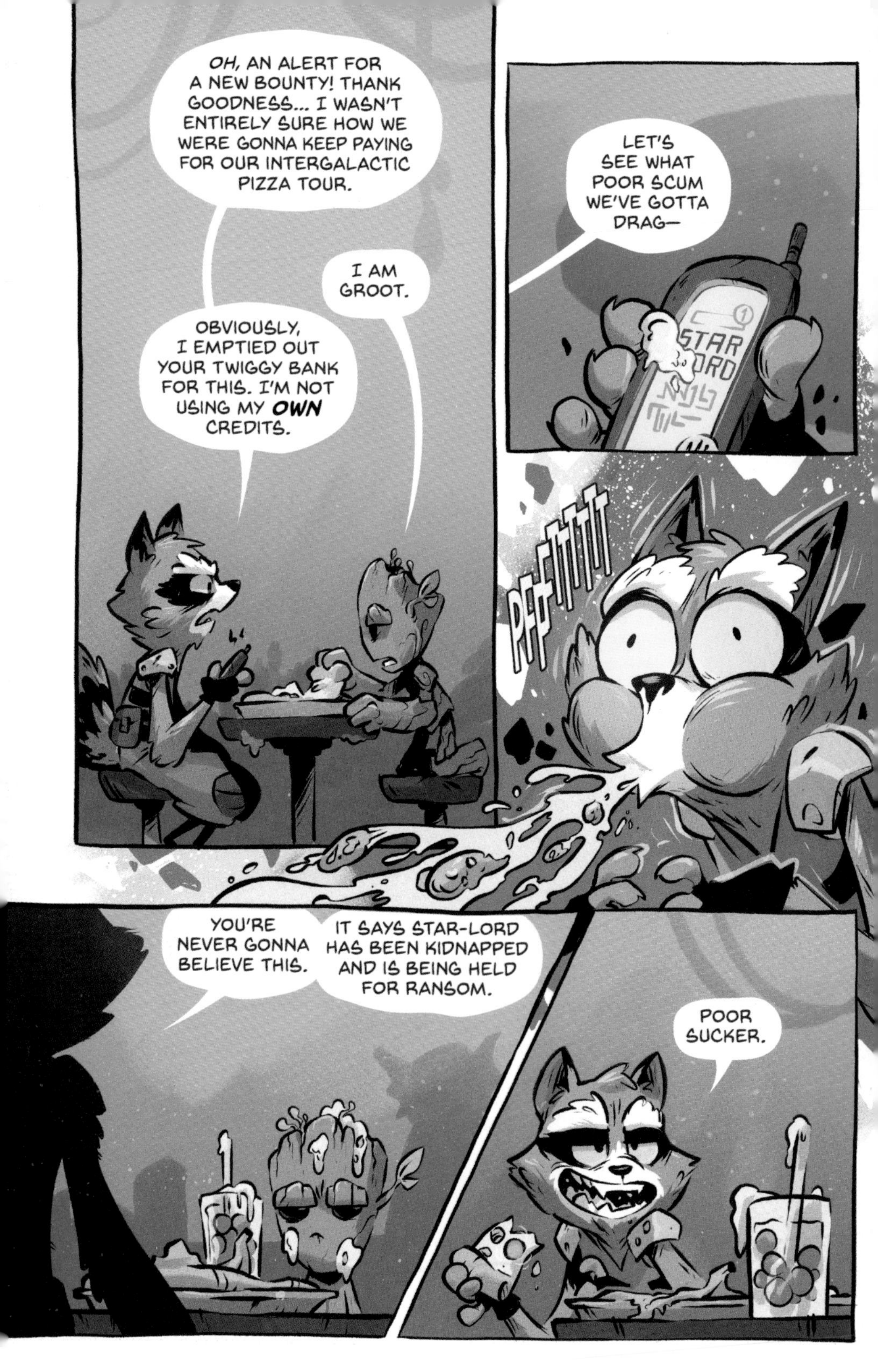
OH, AN ALERT FOR A NEW BOUNTY! THANK GOODNESS... I WASN'T ENTIRELY SURE HOW WE WERE GONNA KEEP PAYING FOR OUR INTERGALACTIC PIZZA TOUR.
I AM GROOT.
OBVIOUSLY, I EMPTIED OUT YOUR TWIGGY BANK FOR THIS. I'M NOT USING MY OWN CREDITS.
LET'S SEE WHAT POOR SCUM WE'VE GOTTA DRAG—
STAR LORD
PFFFTTTTT
YOU'RE NEVER GONNA BELIEVE THIS.
IT SAYS STAR-LORD HAS BEEN KIDNAPPED AND IS BEING HELD FOR RANSOM.
POOR SUCKER.

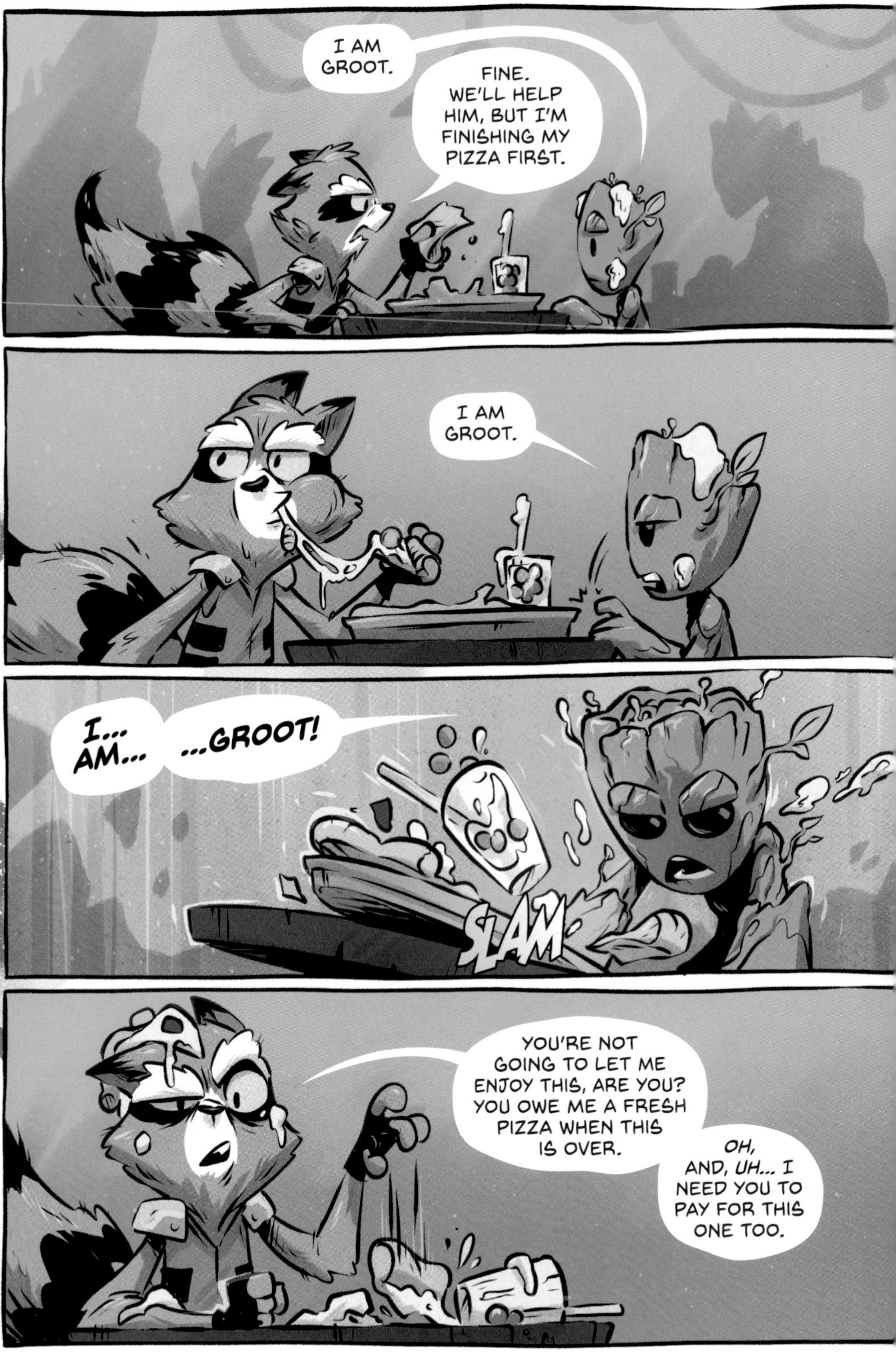
I AM GROOT.
FINE. WE'LL HELP HIM, BUT I'M FINISHING MY PIZZA FIRST.
I AM GROOT.
I... AM...
...GROOT!
SLAM
YOU'RE NOT GOING TO LET ME ENJOY THIS, ARE YOU? YOU OWE ME A FRESH PIZZA WHEN THIS IS OVER.
OH, AND, UH... I NEED YOU TO PAY FOR THIS ONE TOO.

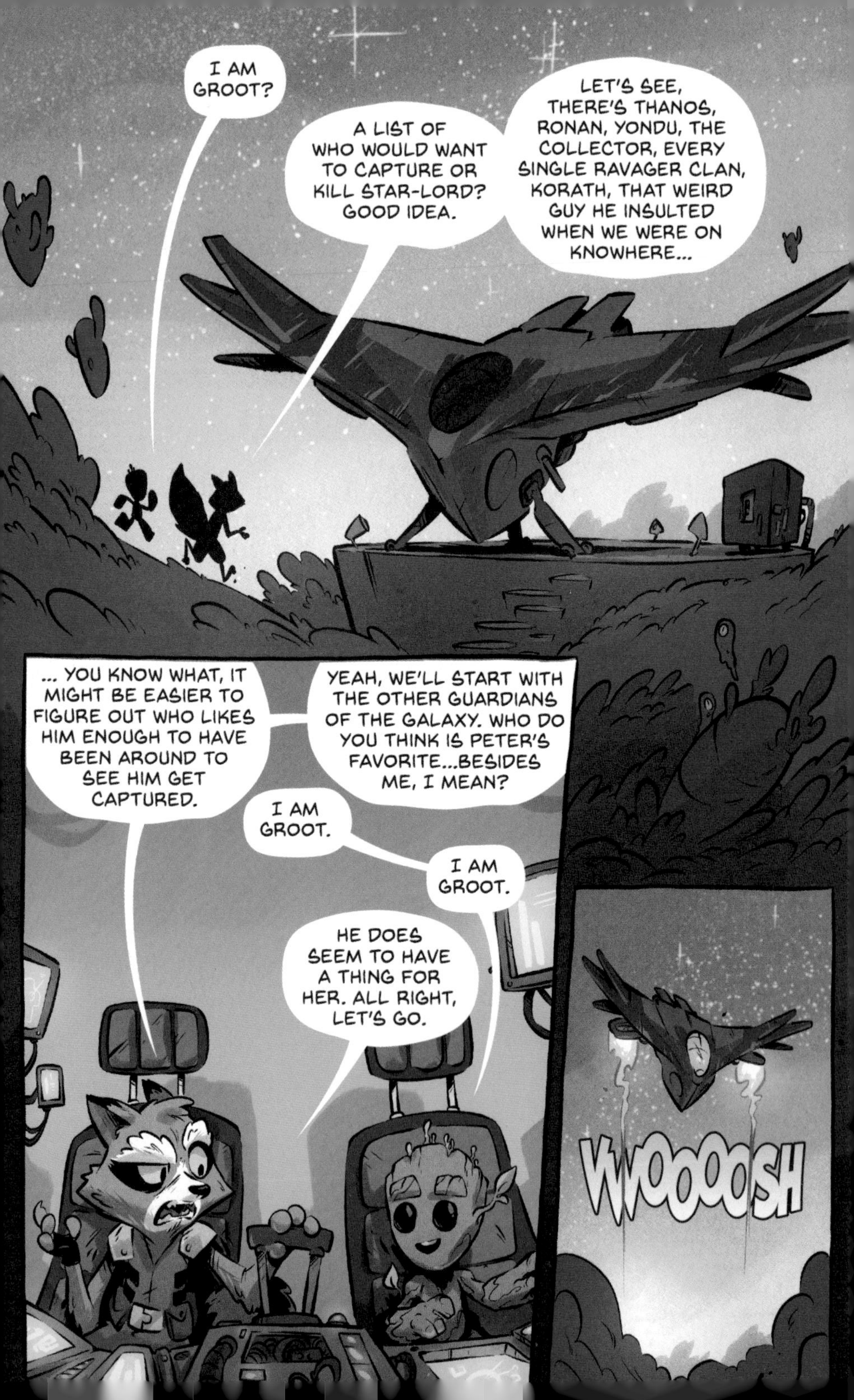
I AM GROOT?
A LIST OF WHO WOULD WANT TO CAPTURE OR KILL STAR-LORD? GOOD IDEA.
LET'S SEE, THERE'S THANOS, RONAN, YONDU, THE COLLECTOR, EVERY SINGLE RAVAGER CLAN, KORATH, THAT WEIRD GUY HE INSULTED WHEN WE WERE ON KNOWHERE...
... YOU KNOW WHAT, IT MIGHT BE EASIER TO FIGURE OUT WHO LIKES HIM ENOUGH TO HAVE BEEN AROUND TO SEE HIM GET CAPTURED.
YEAH, WE'LL START WITH THE OTHER GUARDIANS OF THE GALAXY. WHO DO YOU THINK IS PETER'S FAVORITE...BESIDES ME, I MEAN?
I AM GROOT.
I AM GROOT.
HE DOES SEEM TO HAVE A THING FOR HER. ALL RIGHT, LET'S GO.
WOOOOSH

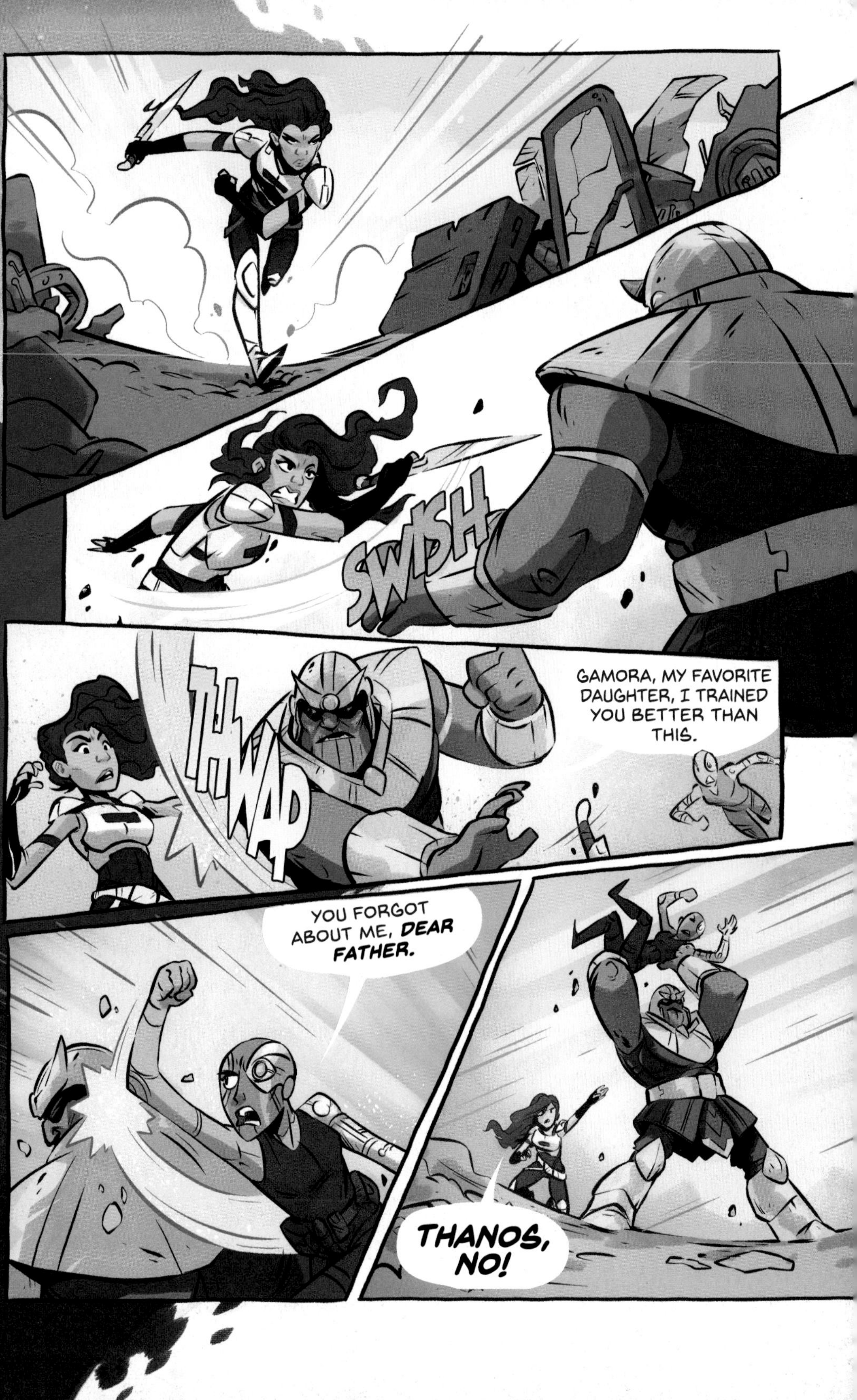

SWISH
THWAP
GAMORA, MY FAVORITE DAUGHTER, I TRAINED YOU BETTER THAN THIS.
YOU FORGOT ABOUT ME, DEAR FATHER.
THANOS, NO!

**STEVE FOXE** is the author of more than fifty comics and children's books for properties including Pokémon, Batman, Transformers, Adventure Time, Steven Universe, and Grumpy Cat. He lives in Queens with his partner and their dog, who is named after a cartoon character. He does not eat ham. Find out more at stevefoxe.com.

**SHADIA AMIN** is a Colombian comics artist currently living in the United States. Her art aims to capture the fun of super heroes, fantasy, and life itself. Her works include BOOM!'s *The Amazing World of Gumball: The Storm*, Oni–Lion Forge's *Aggretsuko*, as well as collaborations on anthologies like *Electrum*, produced by the Alloy Anthology and published by Ascend Comics, and *Votes for Women*, published by Little Red Bird Press. Burgers are to her what hot dogs are to Spider-Ham.